Harley needed ⟨...⟩ ⟨n⟩ot **the way her bo**⟨dy⟩ ⟨had reacted impulsive⟩ly **when she met** ⟨Ryker.⟩

He was off-limits! That way there was no risk of a broken heart. Like what had happened with Jason…

But it had been some time since she'd had that kind of surface-level physical attraction to a man. Clearly Ryker Proulx was dangerous to her heart, and even though he was technically about to become her neighbor, at least she could try to keep him at arm's length. The only time she had to interact with him was if she saw him on the property or if he needed her at the clinic.

It would be totally professional.

And anyway, she liked Michel too much to get involved with Daphne's widower, never mind what had happened with the last vet she fell in love with. She was never, ever going to date a veterinarian again.

No matter how hot the vet really was!

Dear Reader,

Thank you for picking up a copy of Harley and Ryker's story, *Tempted by the Single Dad Next Door*.

When my editor suggested that my next book be about a veterinarian, I was all over that. I got to include animal friends I know personally. Some are gone and some are still with us, like my doggo, Willow, who has a starring role.

Harley is a lot of me. Burned-out by the city and just in love with her farm and country life. Unlike me—I was never jilted. Harley isn't sure she can trust her heart with someone again. Until a certain very tempting single dad moves in next door.

Ryker is another one of my favorite heroes. He's this amazing single dad who just wants the best for his son, who is struggling since Ryker's wife passed two years ago. They come to her hometown for the summer to heal. Ryker was not expecting to find love in small-town Ontario.

I hope you enjoy Harley and Ryker's story!

I love hearing from readers, so please drop by my website, www.amyruttan.com.

With warmest wishes,

Amy Ruttan

TEMPTED BY THE SINGLE DAD NEXT DOOR

AMY RUTTAN

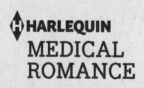

HARLEQUIN

MEDICAL
ROMANCE

HARLEQUIN®
MEDICAL
ROMANCE™

Recycling programs
for this product may
not exist in your area.

ISBN-13: 978-1-335-59532-4

Tempted by the Single Dad Next Door

Copyright © 2024 by Amy Ruttan

For questions and comments about the quality of this book, please contact us at CustomerService@Harlequin.com.

Harlequin Enterprises ULC
22 Adelaide St. West, 41st Floor
Toronto, Ontario M5H 4E3, Canada
www.Harlequin.com

Printed in U.S.A.

Born and raised just outside Toronto, Ontario, **Amy Ruttan** fled the big city to settle down with the country boy of her dreams. After the birth of her second child, Amy was lucky enough to realize her lifelong dream of becoming a romance author. When she's not furiously typing away at her computer, she's mom to three wonderful children, who use her as a personal taxi and chef.

Books by Amy Ruttan

Harlequin Medical Romance

Portland Midwives
The Doctor She Should Resist

Caribbean Island Hospital
Reunited with Her Surgeon Boss
A Ring for His Pregnant Midwife

A Reunion, a Wedding, a Family
Twin Surprise for the Baby Doctor
Falling for the Billionaire Doc
Falling for His Runaway Nurse
Paramedic's One-Night Baby Bombshell
Winning the Neonatal Doc's Heart
Nurse's Pregnancy Surprise
Reunited with Her Off-Limits Surgeon

Visit the Author Profile page
at Harlequin.com for more titles.

For all the doggos, kittens, chickens, horses, cows and alpacas I know and love. Each animal in this book represents an animal who owned my heart or owned friends' and family's hearts. A special shout-out to my doggo, the best writing buddy ever, Willow. You are the bestest girl.

Special thanks to Christine for suggesting the cat rescue name after I tried to generate a random name, with horrible results. Thanks for laughing it off with me and coming to *my* rescue.

Thanks to Cathryn for our shared cockerels.

And thanks to my sister-in-law Theresa, vet extraordinaire. You are an inspiration and this former city mouse loves you.

Praise for
Amy Ruttan

"*Baby Bombshell for the Doctor Prince* is an emotional swoon-worthy romance…. Author Amy Ruttan beautifully brought these two characters together making them move towards their happy ever after. Highly recommended for all readers of romance."

—*Goodreads*

CHAPTER ONE

"DON'T LOOK AT me like that!" Harley Bedard stared down into the big, round, saucer-sized brown eyes of her black-and-silver-colored cockapoo. The only reason Willow was staring at her like that was because Harley was finishing up her quick breakfast of a scrambled egg before starting her morning rounds. Willow always begged for eggs, cheese, chicken, tuna. Basically anything she ate, her dog wanted.

Badly.

Willow shifted, but her gaze was still intense. She stuck out her little pink tongue, wetting her black nose and silvery beard.

Repeatedly.

Harley groaned, but smiled at her goofy little dog. It was hard to resist that adorable face. She held a piece of scrambled egg in her palm and Willow eagerly ate it up.

"Don't say that I don't do anything nice for you," Harley muttered as she patted and scratched Willow's ear. The dog sneezed a couple of times, her feathery tail wagging. "You ready to do our chores?"

Willow sneezed again, shaking her head.

She took that as a yes.

There was a lot to do today. She had to check

on the dogs that were in the kennel. Today wasn't a doggy day care day, so there wouldn't be an influx of clients with their pups driving down her gravel lane, but she did have a grooming session booked in. Her client had three dogs known as the wild bunch, so she tried to schedule that groom on a day when doggy day care wasn't running. Her friend Christine, who ran the local cat rescue, needed her help assessing a new load of kittens and older cats that had been dumped, and then there was a summer renter coming to sign a lease for the tiny home that she had on the other side of her yard behind the chicken house. When she bought the property three years ago, the small cabin had already been there. She'd refurbished it. Usually, she would get the odd tourist who wanted to be in the heart of Huron County for a couple of weeks and loved her little guest home tucked away on her thirty acres just outside of Opulence, Ontario. This time it was different. The house was booked for the whole summer.

The person renting her property was the son-in-law of local vet Dr. Michel Van Dorp. He was semiretired and didn't hide the fact that he wanted said son-in-law to take over his practice.

The vet clinic was integral to this part of Huron County as it was an agriculture community. Harley worked there when needed as a veterinary technician. Only when she had the time, though. Her kennel and grooming business were growing larger every year. Thankfully, she had hired help.

A new vet and a revitalized clinic would be so good for the community. Michel wanted to keep working, Harley knew that, but he couldn't keep up. He was getting older, and his health hadn't been the best since his daughter, Daphne, died two years ago.

Daphne had only been three years older than Harley. It shocked everyone when she died, and it nearly killed Michel.

He had been trying to retire for five years and had brought in other vets, but none of them stayed. People from the city said they liked country life, but they liked it when it was sunny and nice and perfect. No one liked delivering a cow in minus forty weather.

It wasn't her business. It was up to Michel to figure it all out. All that was within her control was her business Cosmopawlitan Opulence, her animals and her summer rental. She had worked out a reasonable deal with Michel to house his son-in-law, Dr. Ryker Proulx, for the summer. Michel was optimistic it could be longer. He was so certain Dr. Proulx would want to stay. Harley had her doubts, she really did. Unless you were from here, no one really stayed.

She knew that firsthand.

Four years ago, she'd fallen for a veterinarian who had come to Opulence. They'd met while Michel was showing him the ropes, and Jason had completely swept her off her feet. He'd said that he loved her and the country life, and after a whirlwind romance, he'd proposed.

She should've known it was too good to be true.

They planned a big, white wedding. Family and friends from all over Huron County came to see her marry her very own Prince Charming. They had dreamed about extending the veterinary practice, buying land, raising a family. Jason had promised so many things.

Love.

Partnership.

Trust.

Harley had bought the most extravagant, sickeningly fluffy white wedding dress. She was so excited for the fairy tale, floating down the aisle to the man of her dreams.

She'd showed up at the church, ready for her happily-ever-after. Except, Jason hadn't.

He'd jilted her at the altar.

When she got back to their home, she saw his bags were packed. Jason came out of their bedroom. He looked apologetic, but clearly his mind was set. She knew that look of determination well.

"Why?" she asked, hugging her arms.

"I'm going to Toronto. I have an opportunity there that I could never get here."

"But what about us?"

Jason picked up one of his bags, hefting it over

his shoulder. "You wouldn't be happy in the city. You weren't even happy in Hamilton, and that's smaller than Toronto. You told me that. It's better this way."

"Is it?" Her voice was breaking.

"It is. You're happy here. You have big plans. I'll be happier in the city, and I have goals that I want to reach. Marriage, right now, isn't a good idea. This was all a mistake."

She didn't respond. She just stood there, numb.

"Bye, Hurley."

It had absolutely crushed her heart.

He didn't want the life they had planned together.

She had been an idiot, and she was never going to get her hopes up again. Never going to put her heart on the line again.

No way.

No how.

She had worked hard to buy her thirty acres on her own after Jason left her. Before she met Jason, when she was working in Hamilton she'd put in hours of overtime, scrimping and saving. Then she returned to Opulence, her hometown, met Jason and they fell in love. She'd taken some of her savings, spending money on the wedding that never happened. After that, she'd tucked anything she made away again. Since then, she'd been building her business slowly in Opulence, and now she'd finally got her feet back under her.

Things were looking up. She had her animals, her farm, that's all she needed.

Wasn't it?

Willow barked, getting her attention, and Harley glanced down at her.

"Message received. We've got work to do." Willow sat down.

Harley slipped on her rubber boots and grabbed her noise canceling headphones, because it got loud in the kennel.

She had to take care of Toby and Gordo, the two dogs currently boarding with her, and then make her way out to her barn to check on her rescue alpacas, Gozer, Vince and Zuul, aptly named after characters in one of her all-time favorite movies. She needed to feed her flock of maniacal chickens that liked to lay eggs all over the place and chase her. She let Willow out, who followed her.

Willow was only twenty pounds, hardly a good security dog. She had been with Harley for eight years now, since she'd helped the veterinarian at the clinic in Hamilton repair Willow's shoddy knees. The runt of the litter, Willow was the one puppy the breeder couldn't sell and Harley promptly fell in love with her.

She made her way to the kennel. As soon as she walked in there Toby and Gordo made it clear they were excited to see her. The headphones helped drown out the excited barks and yips. She loved it when dogs were so happy to see her, but her eardrums didn't love it so much.

"Come on," she called out over the excitement. As she opened the door to the fenced backyard Gordo, Toby and Willow all bolted. Thankfully, the three of them got along so she didn't have to separate them. She refreshed their water and put food in their bowls.

She'd let the dogs play while she made her way to her alpacas. Her rescue alpacas snuffed and stood up in their pen, happy to see her. Harley made sure the pasture gate was secure before she opened the stall door.

Once everything was done, she let the alpacas out to munch on fresh grass. Vince, Zuul and baby Gozer trotted from the barn, frolicking in the morning sun, while she grabbed a pitchfork to muck out their stall.

"Bonjour." There was a gentle tap on her shoulder from behind.

Harley screamed, tossed the pitchfork to the floor, spinning around to grab the lapels of the stranger, meaning to flip the guy, but instead she slipped on some excrement and fell into a pile of dirty hay. The stranger fell on top of her, or rather between her legs, landing with an "oof!"

Harley ripped off her headphones. "Who the hell are you?"

Intense gray eyes, with a hint of yellow, met hers as he shook dark hair from his face. Her breath caught in her throat, her face prickling with a rush of heat as their gazes locked.

Her heart skipped a beat and she forgot for one fraction of a second that this guy she had just tossed to the ground, who was lying almost on top of her, was in fact a stranger.

"I'm Dr. Ryker Proulx. Your tenant for the summer," he said, climbing off her.

"Oh!" Of course.

She had just tried, very unsuccessfully, to Krav Maga her new renter. Hopefully, he wouldn't give her little rental a bad Yelp review.

She was a bit taken aback. She had never met Michel's son-in-law before.

Daphne had moved to Montreal after university and got married when Harley had been in school. Like a lot of people who left their small town for greener pastures, Daphne had never returned other than to visit family.

Looking at her husband, Harley could see why.

There was no doubt in her mind Ryker was handsome, but she'd been bamboozled by good looks before.

"Sorry! Couldn't hear you." She groped around in the straw to find her headphones, holding them up as if to say ta-da.

At least she didn't say that out loud.

"See?" she said, wanting to point out that she didn't just pull random guys on top of her in the barn. "I didn't hear you arrive."

Ryker brushed some of the straw off his shoulder. "I figured as much."

"Welcome," she blurted out, still sitting in a pile of alpaca poo.

Oh. My. God. Harley, get ahold of yourself.

Her brother David always said she rambled and blathered around dishy men. So did he. She could feel the warmth of the flush rising up her neck to her cheeks. It was the ultimate tell in the poker game of trying to hide your attraction for someone you just met.

She sucked at the card game too.

A small smile lifted his lips. He held out his hand to help her up. She took it, her pulse quickening, a knot starting to twist in her belly as he pulled her up. He was taller than her, and her heart raced as she looked up at him.

Ryker was exactly her type. His dark hair was longer, but not so long that it brushed the top of his shoulders. His generous mouth was set in a hard line, as he gazed around her barn. There was a hint of a five o'clock shadow on his chiseled jaw.

He was dressed in a black leather jacket, a white T-shirt and well-fitted jeans that had not seen a day's work in the field. His black leather boots were polished too.

Everything about him screamed city, that he didn't belong in Opulence, and that further solidified her belief, in that moment, that he would not be staying. He was a summer visitor.

"Shall we go sign the agreement?" Ryker suggested.

"Yes. Is Michel here?"

"*Oui.* He was knocking on your door when I saw you slip into the barn," he replied in a distinct French-Canadian accent.

"Okay." It wasn't the best way to meet a new tenant, throwing him into a pile of poop, but it was what it was. She quickly made her way out of the barn and saw Michel standing by his red pickup truck.

"There you are!" Michel exclaimed.

"You're early," she replied, hoping Michel didn't notice that his son-in-law was covered in straw, dirt and manure.

"I thought you might be up," Michel said brightly as she approached his truck.

"I'm always up early." She grinned. "I am glad you swung by. I have a busy day. I have to go down to Blyth and help out at the cat rescue this afternoon."

"I figured as much. I heard they got a bunch of strays in," Michel said.

"They did," she confirmed, looking back over her shoulder at Ryker uneasily. He was still wiping off straw and dried crap.

"Harley, I would like to introduce you to my son-in-law, Dr. Ryker Proulx from Montreal. Ryker, this is the vet tech I often bring in and as you know, she's your landlord for the summer too!"

Ryker turned to her, those gray eyes fixing on hers with a momentary widening of shock and a quick travel up and down her person that sent a shiver of anticipation through her.

"The vet tech?" Ryker asked.

Michel nodded. "Yep."

Her gaze locked with Ryker's again. He still looked surprised. She knew she looked a fright, wearing her baggy overalls, rubber boots that came up to her knees, a grungy tank top, and her hair barely brushed and put up in a very large top knot. At least they were both covered in alpaca crap and straw.

Get a grip.

Her inner voice was right. Who cared what she looked like? And the way she looked had nothing to do with her ability as a certified and well respected veterinary technician.

She wasn't here to impress him, even though there was a part of her deep down that wanted to… She locked that niggling thought away. Dr. Proulx was her tenant, a widower and Michel's son-in-law.

Most important, Harley was fairly certain Ryker was here temporarily, and she wasn't interested in dating anyone. Especially someone who wasn't staying.

"Pleasure to meet you properly, Dr. Proulx," Harley said, clearing her throat and shaking all those thoughts away as she extended her hand.

Michel's eyes widened as he realized the state she and Ryker were in. "What happened?"

"I surprised her. We both took a tumble," Ryker explained coolly, accepting her proffered hand. She felt a little zing of warmth shoot up her arm and quickly pulled her hand back, annoyed at her reaction to him.

"Well," Harley started, clearing her voice. "I just need to go let Toby and Gordo back in their kennel. The tiny home is on the other side of the yard. It's unlocked, so do have a quick look around and make sure it's what you want and I'll meet you both back here."

"Sounds good, Harley," Michel responded.

Harley needed to focus on her work and not the way her body had reacted so traitorously when she met Ryker. He was off-limits. That way there was no risk of a broken heart. Like what happened with Jason.

However, it had been some time since she had had that kind of physical attraction to a man. Ryker Proulx was dangerous to her equilibrium and even though he was technically about to become her neighbor, at least she could keep him at arm's length. The only times she had to interact with him would be if she saw him on the property or if he needed her at the clinic.

It would be totally professional.

Besides, she liked Michel too much to get involved with Daphne's widower, and after what happened with the last vet she fell in love with, she was never, ever going to date a veterinarian again.

No matter how hot the vet was.

Ryker watched Harley walk away. He had spied the fences of the kennel and saw the sign at the head of the driveway. Cosmopawlitan Opulence.

He'd cringed at the cutesy name, but Michel had huge respect for Harley.

Honestly, when Michel had mentioned that he had a friend who had thirty acres, ran a kennel and owned a tiny home that they rented out, he had assumed the woman was closer to Michel's age. He had been shocked to see a younger woman, maybe in her early thirties, running such a successful business and owning quite a bit of farmland.

He was also taken aback by her stunning beauty, even covered in muck and straw. She looked a wreck in baggy overalls and her golden hair tied up in a messy bun, but when their gazes locked, his heart had beat just a little bit faster and when he landed on top of her, his blood had heated at the brief touch. Yet it was her eyes that had shocked him. They were so blue, and he saw a spark of strength buried deep in that cerulean color, before his gaze traveled down to her soft, pink, plump lips. For one brief second, he thought about what it would be like to kiss them.

Only for a brief moment, and then the guilt overcame him, for a split second.

Daphne had been gone for two years. She had been his world, they had a beautiful son, Justin, and then when they thought they were pregnant with their second, her pregnancy turned out to be ectopic. Her tube ruptured and she bled out so fast there was nothing to be done.

All he could do was take care of their son.

The problem was, they were isolated in Montreal.

After Daphne died Ryker had thrown himself into work and taking care of Justin. Friends had drifted away. Even Justin's friends, because he no longer wanted to play sports or do anything without his dad.

So no, maybe not fully isolated, but it mostly was just Justin and him.

He had no family left. Ryker had been an only child, and his parents were dead. They had talked for a couple years about moving back to Daphne's hometown, to be near her parents and so Justin would have cousins who lived close by.

It would be family, but now Daphne was gone and he wasn't completely sure that he could leave everything behind and live here. Montreal was his home. Justin's home. He'd told Michel he would stay for the summer, to see how it worked out.

The truth was Justin was struggling. Montreal reminded him of his mom and he never let Ryker far out of his sight. Ryker was actually surprised that he'd been able to come here to sign the lease, but Nanna was occupying Justin for now. He was hoping the summer here in Opulence would help the boy heal.

Justin thought they were on an extended summer vacation. He was nine and just so excited to be near his grandpa, his nanna and some cousins. Ryker hadn't seen Justin this happy in so long.

To keep himself busy, Ryker had offered to work for his father-in-law. A small-town vet practice would be a break from the hustle and bustle of a city practice.

So when Michel offered up his friend's tiny home as a rental for them, Ryker thought it was perfect, until he learned that the so-called friend was a good-looking, sexy blonde. Maybe, he needed to find another place to rent.

"Well, let's go see the place. It's just on the other side of that coop," Michel said, walking toward the chicken house in question.

"Maybe we should find somewhere else," Ryker said cautiously.

Michel paused and raised his bushy eyebrows. "This is the closest rental to the vet clinic, at a decent price. There's not much for rent in Opulence."

"Right. So you've said," Ryker groused. He had no choice.

"I know Harley looks a little rough around the edges, but she is a smart, savvy businesswoman and part-time vet tech."

"Part-time?" Ryker asked, all too aware that Harley was not only his landlord, but someone who would be working with him.

"Yes. She works sometimes at the clinic. Just part-time as she's really busy here. There's a shortage of good, reliable and bondable pet services. When I'm not at the vet clinic, people do have to drive thirty, sometimes forty minutes. There are wait lists for groomers."

Ryker was shocked.

Wait lists?

He took for granted the city life, where there was always some artistic doggy or pet spa popping up.

"Besides," Michel said, interjecting through Ryker's thoughts of doubt. "This is the only place that has a lease term that you're looking for. The rest are cottages that rent an enormous amount week to week and are mostly fully booked, sometimes a year in advance."

Michel was right. Ryker was stuck. The vet tech and working at the clinic part worried Ryker, but if she worked with him, then she was definitely off-limits. As long as he compartmentalized her in his mind like that, maybe this could work out.

He couldn't tell Michel his real hesitations for wanting to stay here. He couldn't let his father-in-law know that for the first time since he lost Daphne he was physically attracted to someone.

That wasn't going to happen.

"D'accord, let's go see this place then."

Michel nodded and Ryker fell into step beside him.

There was frantic barking and he glanced over his shoulder, pausing to watch as Harley opened the door to the gated play area of her kennel. Two dogs came bounding over to her, tails wagging happily, before finding their respective places to do their business. Harley's little dog trotted in front of her.

She had her noise canceling headphones back on. She was tossing balls and other soft toys at the dogs as they bounded around happily outside, running all around her and demanding her attention.

Harley was smiling and laughing as she took a ball from the big, horse-like dog and tossed it again. It was clear she was passionate about what she did, and Ryker couldn't help but smile, watching her.

That passion was what he felt for animals, too.

Before he got married, he had a red setter that had been his best friend. Daphne had loved his dog, Temart, too and even in his old age the dog had been so protective of Justin as an infant. A lump formed in Ryker's throat as he thought of his old dog.

These were memories he thought he'd locked away, but watching Harley out in that kennel with those happy dogs brought those memories rushing back and it overwhelmed him. There was a part of him that wanted to join in on the fun—he couldn't remember the last time he'd let loose and tossed a ball to a dog. It surprised him how she affected him so.

Someone he barely knew.

Don't think about her. Don't let her in.

And he had to keep reminding himself of that. All he had to do was rent a place from her and possibly work with her on a professional level. That's it. Just because he was attracted to her, it didn't mean anything. He was not opening his heart to the prospect of pain.

He couldn't deal with that kind of loss again. It was too risky.

All that mattered to him in this world was Justin's happiness.

He'd loved and lost. And he was never going to go through that again.

CHAPTER TWO

ONCE SHE HAD got somewhat cleaned up, taken care of the dogs and got them settled back into their kennels, or doggy suites as she liked to call them, Harley made sure they both had a nice pupsicle to smooth over the wound of being put back inside. Even Willow got her own doggy suite and pupsicle so she wouldn't be underfoot as Harley went out to the tiny home and dealt with the lcase.

That's if the fancy veterinarian from Montreal thought her summer rental was good enough. She laughed to herself as she thought about how she sounded like some of the older members of Opulence, casting derision at the out-of-towner. And she felt slightly bad for ruining his nice clothes.

When was the last time she dressed up? She couldn't remember.

Life on her farm, running her business and dealing with animals, didn't leave her too much time to go out. And she had never been one for dance clubs, or even a girls' night. She was a bit of a loner.

Her phone buzzed. It was her older brother, David.

"Yo," she answered, stepping out of the noisy kennel.

"Hey, Nerd," David replied. "Wondering what you're up to today."

"Cat rescue, a groom and dealing with a summer tenant."

"Usual then."

"Summer tenants are hardly usual," she remarked.

"Oh! I missed that part. A summer tenant?" David asked, intrigued.

"Michel's son-in-law from Montreal."

"Is he cute?" David asked.

Her stomach did a little flip. *That was an understatement.*

"No," she blurted out.

"Liar," David chuckled.

"Do you actually need something, David, or are you just calling to pester me?"

"Yes, I do. My vet's away. I'm dealing with a horse that has a gastric ulcer. He's on omeprazole, but he's still not wanting to eat. Any suggestions?"

Her brother and his partner owned a horse ranch up near Inverhuron. They bred racehorses and were quite adept at minor equine medicine. They were a fully equipped operation.

Harley frowned. "How long has he been on the omeprazole?"

"For a couple of weeks."

Harley frowned. "His stomach could still be irritated. There's not much I can do over the phone. You'd have to check with a scope to see if the stomach has healed, but it could also be a case of his being afraid to eat."

David sighed. "Afraid? He could be."

"Alfalfa. You got any?"

"Yeah."

"Hand feed him. I also heard, once, beet pulp, but you really have to let it soak in the feed for at least twenty-four hours. I can't come up today, but I could come tomorrow. Do you need me to come?"

"No. It's okay. I know you're swamped. I'm going to try those suggestions and see if it helps him. Our vet will be back in a couple of days, before he goes on his next whirlwind vacation," David said.

"Vacation, what's that?" She laughed dryly.

"Something you need to take once in a while."

She knew it, but when would she have time? At least David had a partner. She was alone here, besides her two employees. "Call me if there any more problems."

"Will do. Love you, brat," David said affectionately, then hung up.

Harley slipped her phone back in her pocket and she hung her noise canceling headphones up over her desk. Her assistant, Kaitlyn, would be coming in soon to watch the dogs while Harley made her way to Blyth and the cat rescue for the afternoon. She glanced at herself briefly in the mirror, just to make sure she didn't have some paw prints or slobber on her, grabbed her tablet with a copy of the lease and then made her way out into the yard, past the chicken house.

Whatever Dr. Proulx decided, she hoped it was quick.

She had other chores to do.

There was a small part of her that hoped he wouldn't stay, because she hadn't been overly excited about how she reacted to him when they shook hands. Dr. Proulx was a danger to her good judgment.

He was so the type of guy she was in to.

Tall.

Dark.

Refined. Even covered in alpaca mess, he was still classier and more sophisticated than her.

Her draw to him reminded her of that instant connection with Jason, and she wasn't going to make that mistake twice. She had learned her lesson.

Have you though?

She thought she had, but work was her life. Maybe that was part of the problem. Perhaps she was lonely. She ignored that little twinge as she approached the tiny house. Ryker and Michel were standing on the covered porch. The deck was something she had added last year, so visitors could enjoy the vista of her seventeen acres of forest and the sound of the small creek that ran across her property. Ryker had clearly slipped off his dirty shoes to look inside and was putting them back on, on the porch when she found them.

Harley winced. Hopefully the leather wasn't

ruined, but she did appreciate him keeping the house clean.

"So?" she asked, coming up the stairs. "What do you think?"

Ryker nodded. "*Très bon*. It will do for my needs."

"Great." She forced a smile on her face. He just lived on the property. She didn't have to provide him breakfast, just had to make sure that he had power and water. They could be neighbors. They didn't have to be friends. "So you have to bring your own bedding."

"That won't be an issue," Michel said. "Maureen has plenty of extra sheets and stuff for Ryker and Justin."

"Justin? Who's Justin?" Harley asked.

"My nine-year-old son," Ryker answered.

And then she remembered. Michel's grandson. Daphne's boy. She hadn't been able to attend the baby shower nine years ago, because she had been in school, but she had sent a gift. A no-sew quilt she had made. It was fleece and had dogs on it.

Everyone in Opulence had been invited.

"Of course," she responded softly. "I remember now. Michel always brags about him."

Michel smiled broadly, nodding and a faint half smile tugged at a corner of Ryker's mouth.

"It won't be a problem with him staying here, will it?" Ryker asked.

"No. Not at all. Sorry if I seemed shocked. It's good to know. Lots of places to ride his bike, if he has one. There's a basketball hoop. It's not overly exciting here."

Ryker smiled at her warmly. "It's perfect."

A blush crept up into her cheeks again. She could feel that flood of warmth. She had to agree with him; her place was kind of perfect.

"Well, I'm glad," she added, not sure what else to say as she stood there grinning like a fool.

"Is that the lease?" Ryker asked, pointing to the tablet in her hand.

Right. The lease. He needs to sign it. Focus, Harley.

"It is." She unlocked the tablet and handed it to him with a stylus. Ryker flicked through the simple contract. His face was serious as he scanned the document, and she just stood there, watching him, rocking back and forth on her heels. Not sure what to do with herself.

Ryker signed it quickly and handed it back to her. "When can we move in?"

"As soon as possible." She reached into her pocket and held out the key. "I hope you enjoy your summer here. I know I do!"

She winced again.

Yep.

Nerd.

Ryker reached out and took the key, their fingers brushing momentarily. Heat coursed through her, and again she quickly snatched her hand back and stuck it in her pocket.

"Thank you," Ryker replied stiffly, holding the key awkwardly.

"Great. Well, I have to go into Blyth in a couple of hours and offer my assistance to some rescue cats."

"Do they need my help?" Michel offered. "I mean, I have a doctor appointment first…"

"No. It's fine. I can handle it," she said.

Michel looked at his son-in-law. "Ryker can go!"

Ryker's eyes widened, and she didn't know what to say. She couldn't say no, but she didn't want to say yes.

"I'll go," Ryker stated, breaking the tension.

"What about your son?" Harley asked.

"He's with his nanna for the day. If I am to work in this community for the summer, I should get to know the local rescues," Ryker said.

Harley was flabbergasted. The new vet hadn't even moved into his home yet and he was offering to come to Blyth. Granted, Michel had offered him up, but he agreed. Albeit reluctantly.

"Well…" Harley stammered. "I have to be there in two hours. Michel knows the address and yeah, it would be great to have you there to meet the rescue volunteers."

Ryker nodded. "Excellent. We better get back home so I can change and then I can grab what I need. Right, Michel?"

"Of course." Michel grinned, then frowned. "Maureen needs your car though, Ryker. I have my appointment, and she promised to take Justin to the beach."

"Ah. That's right." Ryker frowned.

Without thinking Harley blurted out, "I can pick you up and take you there."

Ryker's eyes widened. "That won't be a problem?"

"Nope. Not at all."

You're being very aggressively friendly.

"All settled," Michel stated brightly. "Thanks, Harley."

"Thank you," Harley replied. "I mean, you're welcome."

She was still stunned she'd offered to go out of her way to pick up a virtual stranger. However, it was good for the cat rescue. A veterinarian volunteering their time was amazing. It would be worth the awkward car ride.

"I'll pick you up in an hour or so," Harley said.

"Sounds good," Ryker replied.

She watched them walk across the yard and get into Michel's pickup truck. She meandered back toward the house to put away her tablet. Michel honked and waved, but Ryker didn't look back at her.

Not that she expected him to.

Ryker could've said no. He was kind of bamboozled into helping out by a well-meaning, but oblivious Michel. Either way she was glad. Her offering up a ride, well, she still didn't understand what came over her when she said that. As Michel drove out the driveway, Kaitlyn's little car turned in and she honked in greeting to Michel before parking in her usual spot beside the kennel.

Harley made her way over to the vehicle. Kaitlyn was eighteen and was saving up money to go to university and then eventually veterinary college. She was Harley's right-hand woman at Cosmopawlitan Opulence.

"Who was that?" Kaitlyn asked excitedly.

"It was Michel," Harley responded sarcastically.

Kaitlyn rolled her eyes. "Not Michel, the dark handsome stranger in the passenger seat."

"Michel's son-in-law and the new veterinarian in town. He's staying at the tiny house with his son. At least for the summer."

"How exciting. Do you think he'll stay for good?"

"No," Harley replied frankly.

Men like Ryker didn't stay in small towns. A day would come when Kaitlyn would leave for school, and Harley seriously doubted she'd come back. Kaitlyn would move somewhere a little more exciting than Opulence.

Barely anyone stayed here.

"Bummer. It'll be some time before I get my degree and can take over."

Harley smiled at her. "You'll do great, I'm sure. I'm going to go put this tablet away, and then I have to go feed the horde of chickens and the alpacas."

Kaitlyn nodded. "Good luck. I like chickens, but

your flock should be storming the beaches of England like some vikings."

Harley chuckled at that image. "You think they need horned helmets?"

"No! They peck my ankles enough." Kaitlyn headed inside the boarding barn and Harley went back to her home. She couldn't stand here in the driveway all day muddling over Dr. Ryker Proulx. She had chores and commitments. She couldn't give an extra second to a man who was only here for the summer.

A temporary resident.

At least, that's what she told herself. Her mind had other ideas.

Why did I agree to this?

Ryker kept asking himself that question over and over in his head as he gathered his gear out of his suitcase along with some equipment that Michel had graciously loaned him. He should've said no, but he didn't have much of a choice since Michel had volunteered him. Giving his time to a nonprofit was a no-brainer, but what was difficult for him was the fact he'd be working closely with Harley. If she was just his landlord, he could avoid her, but she worked in his sphere.

A vet tech.

Now, he'd be traveling in a car with her. He wasn't sure how long it was to get to Blyth or this rescue. Could he even remember how to make small talk? These days he either talked work or talked parenting with other people. He'd completely lost touch with adult chatting with friends who either weren't married or didn't have kids.

His whole life had become work and making sure Justin was okay.

Which he wasn't.

Justin rarely played anymore. He was always by Ryker's side and was struggling in school. It was like Justin was afraid to let him out of his sight.

Ryker hoped this summer would get Justin out of his funk and help him remember how to play. He hoped it would heal him before they headed back to Montreal.

Working at Michel's clinic would be a slower pace than the city, but at least he could do something useful and spend more time with family.

He'd thought this was going to be an easy summer. Until he met Harley.

When Ryker had got back to his in-laws' small condo, where he and Justin had been couch-surfing for the last couple of days, he'd showered and changed into an older pair of jeans and a flannel shirt, and now there was nothing to do but wait for Harley to pick him up.

Sure, there were beautiful women, but there was something about Harley that he quite couldn't put his finger on, that drew him in. Ryker found it disconcerting.

Extremely so.

He paced on the driveway and for one brief moment he thought of backing out. Which would look terribly unprofessional. It's not like he could run and hide. She knew where he lived, at least for the summer.

Ryker chuckled to himself at the absurd idea of running away and hiding just because he was attracted to Harley and would be working closely with her.

A blue pickup truck pulled into the driveway and Harley waved at him from the front seat.

Did everyone drive pickups around here?

His luxury sedan already stuck out like a sore thumb with his Quebec license plate in a sea of dusty trucks and Ontario plates. He loaded the gear into the bed of her truck. He opened the passenger door.

"Howdy! Ready to save cats?" she asked forcefully.

"That's enthusiastic," he teased.

Pink tinged her cheeks. "Well, it's a great rescue. You have to be enthusiastic about that!"

"I'm sure." He buckled up and she pulled away from Michel's house.

An awkward silence descended between them. Ryker sneaked a glance at Harley. She still had her blond hair piled on the top of her head, but it was now neatly braided into a bun. The rubber boots were gone and replaced by sneakers, and she was wearing scrubs that were branded with her doggy boarding facility. They were covered with little cartoon animals in various poses, attending a spa. A couple of poodles were getting their "hair done," and he saw a cat doing yoga poses. There were many more little pets on her scrubs, but he had to tear his gaze away before she thought he was staring at her.

Which he was.

And it wasn't just the cartoon animals that were drawing his gaze. The scrubs were loose, but not as generous as the overalls she was wearing this morning.

He could make out the curve of her hips, the swell of her breasts, which was not what he should be focusing on now. Especially as she was doing him a favor by driving him.

It was inappropriate.

"Thanks again for picking me up," he said, breaking the silence.

"It's no problem. Thank you for volunteering your time. It really is a big deal with this community. Rescues are a great thing."

She was talking a mile a minute, and he couldn't help but smile as she quickly glanced at him. She grinned, a wide, fake, set smile that didn't reach her eyes.

Not that he could blame her. They hadn't really talked much so far. He'd been a bit aloof with her. It was easier that way.

For who?

He ignored that thought. It was best he kept everything professional. He didn't need to make friends with her. All he had to do was be cordial. He'd see to these cats quickly and put Harley out of his mind. Still, she agreed to pick him up. He couldn't be a jerk.

"Thanks again for agreeing to help out," she said.

"Well, I think you mean thank you for being volunteered by Michel, *oui*?"

Harley smiled, that cute little grin that made his heart beat just a bit faster. "Right. Still, it's appreciated."

"You've thanked me three times, but again, it's no problem. You're right, rescues are important."

"I tend to repeat myself. A lot. Especially around people I don't know. So my apologies for the over-abundance of gratitude. I mean, you could be terrible and I'll regret thanking you later."

Ryker chuckled again. "You have so little faith in me then?"

"Of course not. I don't know you at all. But I've been around vets. Good and bad."

"I assure you, I'm good."

"Do you have your own practice?" she asked.

"No," he said, sighing. "It's expensive to manage and run a clinic in Montreal. I am an associate at a busy urban clinic."

He also didn't have time to run his own practice, not when Justin needed him.

"Running a business takes a lot of time. For sure. I know."

"You managed to buy a business and a farm. It's impressive."

Pink flooded her cheeks again. "Thanks."

"That's four times now," he teased.

He liked the way she smiled at him. It made him want to get her to smile more, to have her blue eyes twinkle. To make her happy.

Get ahold of yourself.

He needed to regain control of these thoughts running through his mind. He was not here to make Harley happy.

"How many cats are we looking at today?" Ryker asked, trying to steer the subject onto business, so he didn't have to make small talk or think about how cute she did look in those ridiculous scrubs.

"Eight."

"Eight?" he repeated, surprised.

"There's also a couple that are feral and most likely could be considered for the feral barn cat program," Harley admitted. "They still need their shots and to be checked out to make sure they're healthy. We'll most likely have to sedate the feral ones, so it's actually good you're here."

"So eight fairly domesticated cats and two or three feral cats?"

"And five kittens."

Ryker's eyes widened. "So, about sixteen then?"

So much for a quiet day. Why did he think summer here would be a slower pace?

This is just a rescue. Rescues are always full.

Harley looked up at the sky and was mouthing numbers silently. "Yes. Is that too much?"

"No. It's fine. I just like to know what I'm dealing with."

They'd be there awhile.

Harley pulled into the parking lot next to a newish looking barn that was very similar to her kennel. It was long, kind of like a modern milking barn, but with walls, instead of open sides for the cattle.

"We're here," Harley announced, parking.

"Looks respectable."

"It is. It's very well run. I'll introduce you to the couple that runs the rescue."

"D'accord." Ryker got out of her truck and they grabbed the gear from the back. He then followed Harley. There was a big sign out front that said Fluffypaws Rescue, and there was a huge cartoon cat painted in the style of chibi. It was all so cutesy. Too cutesy for his sensibilities, but he knew that would help attract potential adopters.

The barn door opened and a blonde woman in kitty scrubs came out, smiling, relief washing over her face. "Harley, thank you for coming."

Harley hugged her. "No problem, Christine. Always happy to assist."

Christine turned to look at him. He smiled and extended his hand. *"Bonjour, mademoiselle."*

"This is Dr. Proulx from Montreal," Harley informed her. "He's Michel's son-in-law who is here for the summer. He wanted to meet you and help out today too."

Christine smiled brightly at him and took his hand. "Pleasure to meet you, and I'm so glad for an extra pair of hands!"

"I'm glad to be of assistance," Ryker answered. He glanced over at Harley, who was smiling warmly at him. There was a genuine warmth, and it made his heart skip a beat. As much as he wanted to keep her at arm's length and keep it professional, he couldn't help but smile back at her. For some reason it made him happy to see her smile so warmly at him and know that he was making her happy right then.

Focus.

He really had to pull himself together.

He wasn't here to please her. He was here to do a job and that was it. The whole purpose of his summer out here in southwestern Ontario was to have Justin near some family. He was hoping the summer here would cheer Justin up. That's it.

He wasn't here to flirt or even think about getting involved with someone. He wasn't going to put his heart on the line. He wasn't going to lose in love.

Again.

His heart couldn't take another shattering. It had hurt too much.

"Let me show you around," Christine said, interrupting his thoughts.

"Please," he said, quickly and tightly locking away his smile.

Right now he had to just focus on the task at hand and that was assessing the cats and kittens. Harley was a vet tech and he was a veterinarian; they were just here to work.

CHAPTER THREE

CHRISTINE SHOWED RYKER and Harley where they could set up and do their work for the afternoon. Ryker was extremely impressed with how the rural rescue was set up and so well run. The barn had a small exam room, which had an exam table and a weight scale. Christine stated she was going to slowly bring the cats in to them from where they were housed in their kennels. He could see the kennels through a window. They were clean and spacious.

In the exam room and supply room there were vaccines and other medicines that he would need, all generously donated by various vet clinics around the county. Even private members of the communities and businesses gave to the cat rescue. He could see names of benefactors listed on a plaque on the wall—and by plaque he meant a beautiful cross-stitch that Christine had stitched herself. She had explained this all during the tour and how she did it to show her gratitude to those who donated and volunteered.

He saw Harley's name there. Just below Michel's. Harley Bedard.

Reading her last name, he wondered if she had French origins too.

You need to pay attention.

Here he was, letting his thoughts wander toward Harley again. He had only known her a couple of hours and he was devoting all this time to thinking about her. What he needed to do was focus on the job at hand.

But it was apparent how well liked and respected Harley was in this community.

"So," Christine stated. "I'll let you two get to work. Harley knows where everything is."

"Merci," Ryker said.

Harley spun around on her heel. "So what's your plan of action?"

"Plan of action?" Ryker asked, cocking an eyebrow.

"Yes. This is the first time we're working together. I need a plan."

"Okay." He ran his hands through his hair, trying to think. "Well, I'll vet the cats and make sure they're healthy."

"Of course. We need veterinarian certifications so Christine and her husband, Dave, can start working on finding foster families or forever families. Or as we like to say, fur-ever."

He grimaced. "Ooh, that's a terrible pun."

"I ramble. Sorry." She shrugged.

"I noticed," he mumbled. "So, we are going to get the cats ready for adoption then. *Oui*?"

"That's the goal for the nonprofit."

"I would assume so." Their gazes locked and his heart skipped a beat. He quickly looked away and tried to focus on getting his equipment ready and not the fact that he was now alone in a room with Harley. Neither of them said anything to each other as they got everything ready for their furry friends.

He found her rambling and her incessant nervous chatter charming. The more he talked to her, the more he liked being around her.

It was distracting.

This is ridiculous.

He always talked to his vet techs. It was all business. So why was he reacting like this? Harley was no different from any other vet tech he worked with. Except she was. Harley was his new landlord, and he was really drawn to her. He thought he was long past this awkward tension with a woman he found attractive.

He had been a fool when he first met Daphne twelve years ago. He had been so awkward when he met her in Guelph at school, and she had laughed at him. They'd fallen deeply in love and never stopped laughing.

Well, he stopped laughing after she died. He couldn't stop the memory from sneaking in.

"Daphne?" Ryker called out. Justin was dragging a grocery bag up the steps.

"Look, Pappa," Justin shouted proudly.

"I see, buddy." He headed back into the house. It was quiet, except the shrill whistle of a kettle.

Where was Daphne?

Ryker set the rest of the groceries down as Jus-

tin dragged the smaller bag in. He made his way to the kitchen and turned off the kettle, then he saw Daphne unconscious, lying on the floor. Like she had collapsed on her way to the kitchen.

"Daphne!" He was on his knees, calling emergency services as he checked for breathing, for any sign of life. There was no pulse.

There was a scream in his head.

"Mama!" Justin cried out. Then he began to sob and there was nothing Ryker could do. He was powerless.

Ryker shook that memory away. He didn't want to think about it today.

"Are you okay?" Harley asked, interrupting his thoughts.

"Fine," he replied stiffly, annoyed that he had let that thought creep back into his mind. Daphne had died two years ago. He thought he had locked all that grief away. He had Justin to take care of. He had spent two years trying to be strong for his son.

This was not the time or place to let that memory back in.

What he needed to do was to keep talking about work.

"So, this feral barn cat program? Tell me about it."

Harley's blue eyes widened, but only for a moment. "Well, it's not called that officially, but basically it's designed for feral cats—cats that don't want to be inside cats and want minimal contact with humans. You provide them shelter outside, a bowl of food and clean water. We neuter and spay them, vaccinate them and all that good stuff, and then they come and go as they please. Local farmers love it. Helps keep down pests."

"It sounds like a good idea. I think I heard a bit about it, but I worked mostly in a city veterinary clinic. There weren't many feral cats that I had to treat."

"Upscale clinic?" Harley teased, a droll half smile tweaking her mouth.

"Why would you ask that?"

"Well, Montreal is a cosmopolitan type of city. Plus you were dressed *très chic* compared to my rustic grunge."

He laughed. He wanted to tell her how cute she had looked in that rustic grunge look, as she called it. "I guess it does serve a more metropolitan type of clientele. Not many feral cats for the barns in Le Plateau-Mont Royal."

"Is that where your clinic is located?" she asked.

"*Oui.*" He nodded.

"Neat. Well, a lot of the cats in this program are found in the city as well. Street cats. It's not just a rural problem."

"Really?" Ryker was surprised. "Well, yeah, I guess I never really saw that. Maybe my clinic was too posh." Now he was teasing, but it wasn't too far from the truth.

Harley smiled at him. "Don't worry about that.

You're not too posh to help here, and that's what matters. It means so much to Christine, Dave, the community and me."

His heart skipped a beat and he smiled at her. "And you? It means that much to you?"

There was a tinge of pink that crept up her slender neck and pooled in her cheeks. She looked away quickly. "Well, animals mean a lot to me and so does this rescue. There's only so much I can do, but having you here today we can get more done."

He nodded, pleased. "Well, as I said, I'm glad to help out and be a part of the community this summer."

That's when he saw that her grin changed just a little bit and the twinkle went out of her eyes. Like she was disappointed that he was only there for the summer.

"Right. Well, I'll go tell Christine to bring in the first cat." Harley quickly exited the exam room.

Ryker sighed. He felt bad for disappointing her, but it was the truth.

Right now, there was nothing permanent about his situation. He was here for the summer. Montreal was his home, but he was glad to bring Justin here. Even for just a couple of months. It was nice to be close to family.

Hopefully to help knock Justin out of his funk.

When he first decided to spend the summer here in Opulence, he had a pretty clear vision in his head: cheer Justin up and help him connect with his late mother like he needed.

Now, looking at Harley and feeling those first stirrings of attraction, something that he never thought he would ever feel again for another person, he wasn't so sure where this summer was going to take him.

All he knew was he had to protect his heart, because he was not staying.

Christine brought in the cats one by one. Harley really wasn't sure how she and Ryker were going to work. That was why she asked him to lay out his plan, so she'd know what to expect. She had trust issues with veterinarians she never worked with before. Michel and Jason had trusted her completely, but other vets that had come and gone, either through volunteering here at Fluffypaws or at the clinic, sometimes treated her as a glorified coffee girl—at least until she stood up to those who doubted her skill, because she knew what she was doing and when Michel wasn't available, she would often step in and help where she could.

She'd taken three years to earn her veterinary tech diploma through a prestigious college, then a year in animal science and then a certificate in grooming and kennel maintenance at night.

Some people, like Michel, had questioned why she just didn't fully become a vet and the truth was because she wanted this. She loved being a vet tech.

She loved grooming and her dream of a farm and her own business.

Harley had worked so hard to scrimp and save so she could buy her own land and run her dream business of Cosmopawlitan Opulence. She didn't need a doctorate or the title to prove anything.

No matter what some other vets thought. Which was why some temporary vets had deemed her as "difficult." Harley didn't see herself as that.

Rambly.

Awkward.

Chatty.

But damn good at what she did.

Ryker had only seen the weird side of her so far, so she was slightly nervous to see how he was going to be when Christine brought in a beautiful orange-and-black cat that had been named Nia. Would Harley be pushed to the side? Or would Ryker actually work with her?

"Can you weigh the cat for me, please?" Ryker asked.

"Sure," Harley replied, relieved that he was apparently going to utilize her skills.

Nia was a love bug, but skittish when Harley took her from the safety of Christine's arms and held her against her chest. Instantly, Nia began to purr.

Ryker grinned; there was a twinkle in his dark eyes as their gazes locked. A little frisson of excitement zinged through her.

"She seems to like you, eh?" Ryker remarked.

"I think so," Harley agreed.

"Maybe you need a barn cat?" Ryker teased as Harley weighed Nia on the scale.

"I have a feeling that this cat is not part of the barn rescue."

"She's not," Christine interjected. "She's a house cat—she was definitely someone's pet. She was found on the side of the road."

"Is there a microchip?" Ryker asked, opening up his laptop to make notes.

"No. There's never a microchip when they come here, but we do microchip them before we send them out to foster or be adopted," Christine stated.

"Would you like that done today then?" Ryker asked.

"Microchipping?" Christine asked excitedly.

"*Oui*," Ryker replied.

Christine beamed. "If you could?"

"I think Harley and I can manage that," Ryker said, returning to his notes.

"I'll leave you both to it. Just holler when you're done with her." Christine slipped out of the room.

"Nia weighs two point nine kilos," Harley stated, picking up the meowing cat once more.

Ryker pressed his lips together in a thin line. "She's underweight, especially if she was a domestic cat."

"She probably lost some when she was abandoned." Harley couldn't help but nuzzle Nia's fur.

"You sure you don't need a cat?" Ryker asked slyly, his eyes twinkling again.

"I like animals. That's obvious. But no, I have enough at the farm already…"

"Does Fluffypaws solicit the cat pictures to see if the cat was lost and is missing?"

Harley nodded as she set Nia down on the exam table. "They try, and they contact shelters and everywhere they can think of, but without a microchip it's hard to track anyone down."

Nia arched her back and rubbed herself against Harley's arm, her little tail ramrod straight and flicking.

Ryker smiled again and chuckled as he reached out to pet Nia's head. *"Comment vas-tu ma chérie?"*

"Did you just ask her how she was?" Harley asked.

"Oui. Actually, I asked 'how you doing, my sweet girl,' because she is very affectionate."

Nia was rubbing herself against Ryker now, and Harley could feel her insides warming by the way he was looking at the cat. Jason may have been charming and swept her off her feet, but he hadn't been this way with the animals.

He'd been gentle with them, but it was all business.

Harley was a firm believer that animals knew when there was a decent human around. They could sense who was kind and caring. Nia obviously liked Ryker, and Harley couldn't help but smile as she watched him examine her.

The way he was gently talking to her and comforting her when she would let out a little meow… He loved animals just as much as Michel did.

Just as much as *she* did.

Their gazes locked once more, and she could feel the warmth creeping back up into her cheeks. She knew that she was 100 percent blushing in that moment. Why did she keep blushing around him?

It was highly annoying.

Well, you're not rambling. Take it as a win.

She looked away quickly, mortified that she had blushed in front of him again.

"She looks healthy. She's been spayed, I would guess about five years ago. So, we can age her at five years, given her teeth and the state of her coat, but that is just an approximation without previous vet records," Ryker said, petting Nia.

"If there were any," Harley mumbled.

Ryker cocked an eyebrow. "She's domesticated."

"Doesn't mean she was actually taken to a vet. Much. She's been spayed, but maybe not regular checkups and vaccinations."

Ryker nodded. "True. We'll give her a series of her regular vaccinations, if you could prepare them, and then we'll microchip her."

"You want me to vaccinate her?" Harley asked.

"Were you not going to do just that before I agreed to come along?"

"Right, it's just usually when a vet is here that's not Michel or…" She paused, because she'd been about to say Jason's name, and she didn't want to think about her ex. Not in this moment and not any moment of the day.

Ryker's eyes widened. "Or?"

"I mean, besides Michel, other volunteer vets just have me fetch things," she said instead.

Ryker made a face, one that looked like he didn't quite believe her. "That is not right. You're qualified?"

"Yes."

"Then you can do it and I will make notes. Have you done a microchip on your own before?"

"Actually, no," Harley admitted. Microchipping was fairly easy and vets she worked with did that job.

"Well, I will show you how. Then when I am not around and no other vet is, you can help the rescue out and do it yourself."

Her heart sunk a bit when he said that he wouldn't be around, and she really didn't know why. She barely knew him and no one really stuck around in Opulence, so why was she so surprised? Why did it bother her so much? He was only here for a short time. The fact he wasn't staying shouldn't affect her, but it did and she was annoyed at herself.

Get it together, Harley. He's showing you a valuable skill.

Ryker held on to Nia while Harley prepared

all the medicine and then grabbed some treats to help occupy Nia from her shots. Ryker petted and soothed Nia as Harley injected the cat for rabies, FeLV and FVRCP, which was a combo vaccine that helped with feline rhinotracheitis virus, feline calicivirus and feline panleukopenia. The FeLV was to help protect Nia against the feline leukemia virus. Next came the Bordetella, which was administered by drops in the nose.

Ryker held Nia's head and she protested. Harley leaned over him, trying not to think about how close he was to her, how she could smell his clean hair, feel the warmth of his skin or how his breath tickled the side of her neck. How her insides were flipping around, her pulse racing and her ears drumming with the beat of her quickened heart rate.

She administered the drops as quickly as she could. Nia sneezed a few times, not liking the feeling of the drops in her nose, but it was important. She needed Bordetella because Nia was boarding with other animals and they didn't want kennel cough to spread through everyone at the shelter. It was highly contagious.

Nia took the vaccines in her stride and Ryker fed her some treats.

He got the easy part of the job.

Harley disposed of the used syringes and the Bordetella eye dropper in the yellow medical waste bin and then washed her hands.

"Can you hold Nia?" Ryker asked. "And I'll grab what's needed for the microchip."

Harley nodded, not making eye contact with him, because her heart was still racing as she recalled how it felt to be so close to him, how her body reacted.

This was not how a professional behaved, and she was annoyed at herself.

Ryker grabbed everything needed, including the little chip that he loaded into a little blue syringe with a long needle and then a scanner to read the chip once it was implanted. The chip itself was the size of a grain of rice.

"Michel lent this to me," Ryker said. "This is the easy part of microchipping."

"What's the hard part?"

"Paperwork." He winked at her.

"I see," she said, chuckling. "So you want me to register it?"

Ryker grinned, a little devilishly, and it made her heart beat a bit faster. "That would be most helpful. First though, you can inject the chip."

He held out the syringe and Harley took it.

"Grab some of the loose skin on Nia's shoulder," Ryker instructed.

"Like this?"

"*Bonne*. Now, insert the needle and inject the microchip. It's very quick."

Harley inserted the needle and Nia barely flinched.

She pushed the depressor of the syringe down and then pulled the needle out.

"That was easy. I don't know why I thought it would be harder." Probably because Jason always insisted on doing it. Even the paperwork, because she wasn't a vet. Back then she never thought anything of it.

Ryker scanned the chip and the information popped up on his computer, everything to register Nia.

"It populates with the chip information," Ryker stated, pointing to the computer screen. "We'll register it all over to Fluffypaws and Christine, then when Nia is adopted it will be transferred over to the new owner."

Harley leaned over him to get a better look at the computer screen.

She was aware again of being so close to him, but when she realized that her breasts were pressed against his back, she froze.

What are you doing?

Ryker's body tensed under hers and she jumped back quickly.

"It looks great. All official and stuff. Registration is so cool," she said.

Really, Harley?

Ryker looked amused. "*Oui.* Very official."

"Do you want me to fill out the information?"

"No. I'll fill this out. Why don't you take Nia back to Christine. Fill her in and then bring the next cat?" Ryker turned and looked back at his computer screen.

"Of course." Harley scooped up Nia and headed to the door.

She had made it awkward and uncomfortable by getting too close.

Ryker had no interest in her, and she needed to keep things professional.

And she certainly didn't want to fall for someone else who might leave. She was not going to put her heart on the line again for anyone.

If she made time to date, she kept it casual and brief.

She had learned her lesson. There were no happily-ever-afters. There were no fairy tales.

Not for her.

Even if she was starting to suspect she secretly still wanted there to be.

CHAPTER FOUR

THEY FINISHED WITH the cats at Fluffypaws Rescue and got into a good rhythm of working together. It was seamless and comfortable. Nice, even. The rest of the cats and the kittens were in fairly good health. Vaccines, drops and other medicines were administered. Other than instructions of what needed to be done and some more microchipping, all banter and unnecessary chatting ended.

It was cool.

It was professional.

Isn't that what you wanted?

Which was true.

Ryker was a stranger. Even if he was Michel's son-in-law, Harley had never met him before today. She only knew him through stories Michel had told her, which hadn't been much. She never got too physically close when she was working, especially with a man she barely knew. What had she been thinking?

She hadn't been. That was the issue.

Ryker had spoken with Christine and Dave about spaying and neutering the cats that needed it at Michel's clinic in Opulence, free of charge—Fluffypaws didn't have the operating room he needed to do it.

Ryker had said that he wanted to win over the

locals, and offering free veterinary services to a beloved cat rescue was the right way to do it. If Harley didn't know any better, she could've sworn Ryker was going to end up with his name on Fluffypaws's gigantic cross-stitch.

The cats for the barn program were too agitated, and Ryker had made arrangements to also have feral cats seen at Michel's clinic for later in the week. They finished at a decent time at the cat rescue, which Harley was relieved about because she had to head home for that grooming appointment. And the sooner she left, the better. The tension was getting to her. She was tired of blushing and rambling on when she did open her mouth.

She groaned inwardly thinking about the mess she had made by pressing her breasts against Ryker's back. By getting too close with a man she barely knew.

It had obviously made him uncomfortable, from the way his spine stiffened, but she was grateful that he'd brushed it off, like nothing had happened.

Harley was kind of mortified by how she acted. She never usually acted that way around men, even if she found them attractive. Not since Jason.

When she met Jason she'd thought he was so sexy, so handsome and charming. The only difference was Jason hadn't backed away from her awkwardness. He had asked her out to dinner the first night they met and completely romanced her.

Physical attraction did not equal love. She knew firsthand.

She had learned how to keep her heart safe and protected, by not putting herself out there.

So why couldn't she stop thinking about Ryker? Probably just because he was the first man since Jason she had been attracted to.

She had to get over this.

Do you? What if you date him and find out?

Harley snorted at that foolish thought. There was list of several reasons she couldn't date Dr. Ryker Proulx.

1. He was her tenant.
2. He was Michel's son-in-law and Daphne's widower.
3. He was a vet.
4. He wasn't staying beyond summer.
5. Because she really just couldn't take another heartbreak.
6. They had to work together.
7. And who said he was interested in her?

She could probably go on and on, but really there was no good reason to even dream of the idea that they could be together. It just wouldn't work.

Why not?

Harley ignored that little voice in her head. After Jason, she never even considered getting back into a relationship. She focused her energy on building her business. And she didn't really have time to date anyway, which was fine by her.

She wouldn't trust anyone else with her heart.

It had taken a couple of years to really get over the embarrassment of being left at the altar, of having her heart broken in front of her friends and family. Wherever she went for the first few months after the breakup, people would give her a sympathetic look or pat her on the back and tell her to cheer up.

People pitied her, and she hated that with every fiber of her being.

So, no. She was not going to fall into that trap again. Ryker was an out-of-towner, which meant all the big red flags for her heart were standing at attention and waving the word *NO*.

She waited out in the parking lot as Ryker made some arrangements with Christine.

"Everything sorted out?" she asked as he loaded a bag in the back of her truck.

"Almost." He hesitated for a moment. "Would you like to get a drink?"

Her breath caught in her throat. She wanted to, but she had a groom.

"I can't. I've got to get you back to Michel's because I have a client. Maybe another night? We could do a barbecue or something." She winced. A drink was a lot different than a dinner.

"A barbecue would be nice," he said, climbing into the truck. "Your place or mine?"

She laughed. "I'm sure we can figure it out."

They both waved at Christine and she started her truck.

"It's peaceful here," Ryker remarked a little way into the drive. "I grew up in the city. My parents didn't have much use for the country."

"Didn't?" she asked, glancing at him. "Did they pass away?"

He nodded. "My father died while I was in school. My mother passed away just after Justin was born."

"I'm sorry." How horrible for him. First his parents and then his wife.

"What about your parents?" he asked.

"Alive. Plus my older brother David. He lives north of here. They're very much into interfering in my life."

Ryker snickered. "That's what family does."

"I'm sure Michel meddles too, since he does with me and I'm not even family."

"You know my father-in-law well."

"He's been my biggest supporter. I hate that he's going to retire."

She pulled into Michel's driveway.

"Thanks for the ride," Ryker said. "I'll see you tomorrow."

"Yes." She nodded quickly.

"Good night." He closed the door, grabbed his gear and headed around the back of Michel's house.

Harley raced back home and as she pulled into

her driveway Ross was waiting for her. His dogs, Mookie, Aspen and Denver were all waiting in the back of his truck. Mookie was an energetic chocolate Lab that thought she was more horse than dog. She loved everyone, but she'd run you over without a second thought. She barrelled through unsuspecting people all the time, but always followed up with a tail wag and a lick.

Aspen was a yellow Lab with a pink nose, elderly and respectful, but she liked to steal loaves of bread and get sick from snarfing them down in one sitting. She was a smart dog, but not when it came to eating food she shouldn't, especially food that would give her stomach troubles.

Denver was the Boston terrier and sort of the alpha hole of the odd little pack of "mutts" that Ross and his wife owned. Denver was a spoiled prince, cute as anything with big googly eyes and a scrunched-up face, but he could be a bit of a dick.

"Sorry I'm early," Ross said as she pulled up beside his truck. "My wife is working late and I have my little girl to pick up. I was just about to bring them in to Kaitlyn."

"No problem. Sorry I'm a little behind. I was at Fluffypaws helping out the new vet."

Ross cocked an eyebrow. "New vet?"

"Michel's son-in-law is here for the summer to help out," Harley explained.

"That's good to know," Ross said, rubbing a hand over his bald head before slamming a Jays ball cap back on. "I hate driving forty minutes to a vet when Aspen eats something she shouldn't."

"Well, maybe he'll stay," Harley offered optimistically. Maybe if Ryker saw how awesome the people were here and how much he was needed, he'd take over the practice. She still doubted it—why would he leave everything he knew in Montreal?—but Ross didn't need to know that piece of information.

Kaitlyn came out with leads and leashed Mookie. Aspen was a smart old gal, and she just followed her energetic little goon of a sister into the barn. Harley scooped up Denver, who snorted at her with his smooshed-up face and sort of rolled his big, bulgy eyes at her in derision at being manhandled.

"Same treatment as usual?" Harley asked, knowing that Ross needed to rush off to pick up his daughter.

"Please. When should I come back?" Ross asked.

"Give me three hours," Harley responded, glancing down at Denver whose buggy eyes were now giving her serious side-eye…which meant that it might take a wee bit longer. "On second thought, can I get three and half?"

Ross chuckled. "Sure. I'll come by after dinner."

He got into his truck and drove away. She carried Denver into the kennel and got him settled with his siblings, so that she could prepare her room for the groom. She liked to take one dog at a time, or else it would be utter chaos. Especially with this group.

The outside security camera chimed that another car was turning into the driveway. She checked her security camera to see that Toby's mom had pulled up in her truck.

"Don't worry, I got it," Kaitlyn called out as she raced by to the reception area. "I can stay late tonight to help with the Ross crew too."

"You're a gem, Kaitlyn!" Harley shouted over her shoulder.

She was really going to be sad when Kaitlyn left, even if it was inevitable.

No one stayed.

Except her.

And even she had left for a time, but only to work toward her dream. She'd always planned to return.

Harley released Willow from her pen, and the little dog trotted along happily behind her, but sneezed a few times to let her know that she wasn't particularly pleased to have been hanging out in the kennel for most of the afternoon.

Not that Harley could blame her.

"Sorry," Harley offered apologetically. "It's been a busy day."

And it still wasn't over.

After her grooms were done, she and Willow would go check on the alpacas and make sure that they were bedded down for the evening and then make their way to the mob of chickens. Willow would usually sit back a fair distance as the chickens were contemptuous and Willow wasn't that much taller than the rooster.

Her last job for the night would be to make sure the rental was ready to go for the arrival of Ryker and his son tomorrow.

Then she could have a late supper, a shower and start this whole process all over again...which just solidified the resolve in her brain that she didn't have time to date, let alone give more than a passing thought to an attractive man.

Her animals, her business and her farm were more important.

Her brain didn't have time for thoughts of romance.

Doesn't it?

Stupid brain.

Ryker wasn't sure what made him ask Harley out for a drink. He dwelled on it as he watched her drive away, needing a moment to collect himself before heading inside to see his son. It had been a long time since he even thought about going out for a drink after work.

Maybe it was because Justin was with his grandparents. It had been hours since his son had last texted him, and even then it had been different from his usual texts, which all worried about where he was.

So he forgot himself and asked Harley out.

It was freeing.

Maybe bringing Justin here would be good for *him* too? Ryker knew he would have a job. Michel wanted him to take over the clinic in Opulence. It could be *his* clinic.

That's absurd.

He couldn't leave Montreal. It was their home. And he certainly couldn't uproot his son unless Justin wanted it.

He shook those thoughts away.

Ryker had texted Michel earlier to confirm a good time to do the remaining feral cat procedures, but Michel had replied that he needed to clear the date with Harley, because she was the vet tech that Michel had hired on an as needed basis. If she wasn't available to help then it was all a moot point, since the other vet techs that he had employed in the past had either retired or moved on to other clinics that could offer them more hours.

Then, distracted, Ryker had completely forgotten to ask her before she drove off.

Maudit.

That was unusual for him. He just got so caught up in being himself around her.

Not a vet.

Not a father.

Just him. It was refreshing. Coupled with the fact he was so drawn to her and he didn't know why.

When Harley had leaned over him, it had caught him off guard only because it had ignited every nerve end in his body. She was so warm, so soft, and he'd resisted the urge to spin around in that office chair and pull her onto his lap. Which was a very bad thought to be thinking about someone he barely knew, but it had crossed his mind. Every touch, every look, everything she said made him like her more and more.

He wanted her and that surprised him. Even though he'd only known her a day, it felt like he'd known her longer. He wasn't sure why.

It was easy to work with her. And he enjoyed her incessant chatter.

Michel had not been wrong. Harley was excellent at her job.

Honestly, he thought she belonged in a clinic full time and he couldn't help but wonder why she didn't continue her studies and become a vet. She had a way with animals.

That's none of your business.

For one brief moment he thought about what it would be like to run the Opulence clinic alongside her.

It thrilled him and terrified him at the same time, but he was being silly thinking this.

Harley wouldn't give up her successful business to work solely with him. No matter how much he would like that.

It wasn't his place to question her, and usually he wouldn't really concern himself with what another person was doing. But for some reason he really did want to know more about Harley. And that was troubling to him.

He'd never thought he would ever really think about another woman again, at all. He'd had passing fancies for women he found attractive, but never acted on them because his whole world was Justin and making sure that his son had everything he needed because he had lost his mother.

Justin needs a family.

Ryker sighed deeply as that thought skittered across his mind. Justin did need a family.

It had been just him, Daphne and Justin in Montreal.

And when Daphne got pregnant with their second, they'd talked about living a simpler way of life. They talked about moving to Huron County, but then Daphne had died and Ryker just threw all those plans and dreams he had made with her away, because it was too painful to think about carrying them on without her.

Yet, here he was, in the place they'd talked about moving to, because Justin was lonely. Justin had been only seven, but the grief was so real for him still. Ryker tried to be everything for Justin, but he saw that his son needed more.

Montreal was a great city. It was their home. He had his career there, and so many precious memories were layered in every fiber of their life in that city. Yet, it was the same here. He had visited Michel and Maureen with Daphne; he remembered her stories as she'd go over pictures.

There had been Christmases in Goderich with Michel, Maureen and Lexi whenever Lexi had flown in from out west.

Daphne's older brother, Tomas, was only an hour away in the city of London, and Tomas had four boys who Justin loved playing with.

Ryker was the foreign one here.

Unfamiliar.

He just hoped this summer could help cheer Justin up. Maybe a trip back here could become an annual thing.

Ryker walked up the driveway of Michel and Maureen's condo, a scmidctached bungalow that was just outside the town of Goderich. It was an adult lifestyle community, which was why Justin and he couldn't couch surf for too long. They couldn't stay the whole summer—neither one of them was fifty-five plus.

The community of condos, like his in-laws' and some larger single modular homes, was on top of the bluff. From Michel's place there was an unobstructed view of Lake Huron and the west coast of Ontario's spectacular sunsets.

The community also had its own private beach and from the beach towels waving in the evening sun, he could tell that Justin and Nanna had had a beach day. Maureen had needed his car to drive down the bluff to the beach.

Michel was on the back deck, and Ryker could see smoke rising from his barbecue.

Oh no.

Michel was a brilliant veterinarian and surgeon, but he was no cook.

"Dang!" Michel cursed.

"Did you burn yourself again, Gramps?" Justin called out.

"Just a small scorch," Michel answered jovially.

Ryker chuckled to himself, spinning his key fob around his index finger as he opened the back gate to head into the backyard, dreading whatever burned dinner Michel was cooking up.

"Pappa!" Justin shouted happily.

Ryker set down his gear and held out his arms as his son, still wearing his swimming trunks and still damp, jumped off the low level deck for a hug.

"You are still damp, my friend," Ryker teased as he set his son down. "Have you turned into a fish?"

Justin laughed. "A little. Gramps told me that you rented us a cottage! Is it on the lake?"

"No, it's close to town. Where your mama grew up," Ryker replied. "It's on a farm though, with dogs, chickens and alpacas."

Justin's eyes widened excitedly. "Really?"

Ryker's heart melted. It had been a while since he had seen Justin this excited.

This happy.

This was a good sign.

He let out an internal sigh of relief. It felt like all

this weight had fallen off his shoulders. There was a faint glimmer of the little boy he remembered.

Unburdened and having fun.

Ryker nodded. "There's a forest and a creek. There's a trail to ride your bike."

"That sounds great! When are we going there?" Justin asked.

"Tomorrow morning." Ryker tousled his son's hair, relieved Justin wasn't upset about moving out of his grandparents' condo. He climbed up the steps of the deck with Justin bouncing up and down excitedly beside him, completely thrilled about the idea of a farm.

"I'm going to tell Nanna!" Justin bounded into the house and Ryker took a scat in a wooden Muskoka chair to watch Michel butcher dinner on the barbecue.

"So, have you cleared a time that Harley can come help you at the clinic for the cats?" Michel asked.

"No. I texted her, but she has not responded."

"She's probably grooming. She mentioned having to groom three dogs tonight."

"Hopefully she'll get back to me," Ryker said offhandedly. He was hoping it could be a simple text exchange so that he didn't have to talk to her, because he could not get her out of his head.

The softness of her skin, the way her breasts had pressed against his back. It had ignited his blood. He had wanted to taste her pink lips and run his hands through her golden hair. It had overwhelmed him, how much he wanted her in that moment, so he'd pulled back as fast as he could.

Yet, even now, just thinking about that, it all came rushing back, lighting his blood on fire.

"I doubt she'll get back to you tonight. She'll have chores. If you need to confirm with her tonight, you might as well drive out there after dinner and talk to her face-to-face," Michel stated, interrupting his thoughts.

"Talk to her?" Ryker asked, surprised.

Michel gave him a quizzical look. "Yes. Is that a problem? I thought you two would get along. You worked well together this afternoon, right?"

"*Oui*. She's competent…and she's…" He trailed off, not sure what to say next. As much as he wanted to keep his distance from Harley, it would be hard to do that when he was living at her farm and working with her and when he apparently randomly asked her out for a drink.

And he wanted to fix an appointment for the cat rescue. He needed to firm up the date for Fluffypaws, and if he had to discuss it with Harley in person, then so be it. Tomorrow was all about moving and making sure that Justin settled in all right. He wanted to answer Christine and let her know about those dates as soon as possible, so he could give his son his full attention tomorrow. He wanted it all sorted and booked, and he didn't want to leave an awkward phone message, so there was no real reason not to go and get the appointment figured out.

Perhaps he could bring some of his things over tonight too, and save them an extra trip tomorrow.

"*D'accord*. I'll go to the farm after dinner."

Michel was chuckling to himself.

"What?" Ryker asked.

"You said she's 'competent.'" Michel made air quotes.

"So?" Ryker asked, puzzled.

"She's more than competent. Don't ever tell her she's mediocre and don't have her fetch coffee."

Ryker smiled. "I know. She warned me."

Michel closed the lid of the barbecue and headed into the house for something.

Ryker sat back in the Muskoka chair and stared out over the lake and the sun that was slowly setting. It wouldn't fully set until well after eight, so it's not like he would be headed to her place in the dark.

Even though he really didn't want to see Harley tonight, he would. He knew deep down the best thing for him to get her out of his thoughts was to keep her at arm's length, and going to her place after dinner was doing the exact opposite of that.

Still, this was a professional discussion. It was work related and nothing more. They would be friendly coworkers. He would keep it completely platonic.

He could do that. Couldn't he?

CHAPTER FIVE

AFTER ATTEMPTING TO eat Michel's rubbery, burned steaks for dinner, Ryker headed over to Harley's farm. He felt somewhat foolish driving out there tonight, especially when he was moving in tomorrow morning, but he really needed to focus on making sure that Justin adjusted to the move, and he wanted to also make sure that everything was set up and arranged for Fluffypaws at Michel's clinic.

There were a lot of moving pieces and Harley was the most important, it seemed.

He had to make sure she had time on her schedule as well. And he was still kicking himself for not asking about it on their drive back to Michel's place.

When he parked in her driveway, he could see that she was outside. The sun was setting behind a line of towering spruce trees, casting a golden orange light across the yard. There was a rustling sound, whispering through the low hanging boughs of the spruce trees. He always liked that sound. It made him relax, and it just made the world feel so serene.

He could listen to the wind in the trees for hours. Maybe it could be peaceful for him and Justin here.

Maybe you could be happy here?

The perfect image was interrupted by a couple

of curses, and he watched the scene outside the chicken house in amusement as Harley attempted to herd a very unruly flock of hens and a couple of roosters. It was anything but the perfect pastural snippet of serenity.

"Cluck Norris Jr., you son of a…" Harley shouted as a large gingery-and-black-colored rooster flapped his wings after her. Then it hit him—did she say Cluck Norris…junior?

"Bonjour," he called out, so he didn't startle her and end up on top of her again.

Would that be so bad?

He groaned at the thought. It wouldn't be, but that's not what he was here for.

Harley's head snapped up, and the chickens took the opportunity to continue their scratching and pecking at the ground instead of heading into the henhouse for the night to roost.

"Dr. Proulx, can I help you?" she asked, surprised.

"Please, just call me Ryker. I prefer that to the formal." Which was true. Only new patients called him Dr. Proulx. Once they got to know him, it was Ryker and that's the way he liked it. It was a bit odd to hear her call him Dr. Proulx. Especially given they were going to be living on the same property and most likely interacting on a regular basis.

As much as he'd like to keep her at arm's length, he wasn't sure how that was going to work out. Not when he needed a vet tech. Friends was a good compromise.

Pink flushed in her cheeks, only momentarily. "Ryker, then. How can I help you?"

"Actually, I need to talk to you about something."

"Now?" she asked, glancing back at her chickens and giving a glare to the rooster who had cornered her.

"If we could. I did drive all the way out here."

"You could've texted." She crossed her arms, stating the obvious. There was a whisper of a smile playing on her lips.

"I did, but you didn't respond and I need an answer sooner rather than later."

"Sure," she replied quickly, but he could tell she was just being polite. She was annoyed that her chore was being interrupted, and he did feel slightly bad. She had changed out of her scrubs and was now wearing overalls, with an oversize purple hoodie that had an outline of Lake Huron plastered on the back.

She stepped over the fence and walked toward him, her arms crossed over her chest. He turned his gaze away so that he wasn't looking at her chest directly, or remembering the way her breasts felt against his back.

He wasn't going there again.

He was here for business, not to think about how adorable she looked in that oversize hoodie or how humorous it was to see her conversing with her chickens.

"Is it about tomorrow?" she asked, breaking through his thoughts.

"Tomorrow?"

"Move-in day," she reminded him.

"What? No," he said. "It's about scheduling a time for you to come into the clinic to help me with the Fluffypaws feral cats. We have to neuter them and sedate them to give them a thorough health check."

"Oh," she said, letting out a sigh that sounded like relief. "I was worried it had something to do with moving in tomorrow. Wondering if you needed boxes or a cart."

"No. I'm good. Move in is still a go."

She cocked her head to the side. "Why didn't you just ask me this tomorrow?"

"Fair point," he agreed, smiling gently. "Honestly, it's because I have to make sure that my son settles here tomorrow, so I need to be there for him. And I thought it would be good to get it on the calendar tonight. I know your business and farm keeps you busy."

A strange expression, almost one of gratitude mixed with surprise washed over her face. "Thanks. Other vets Michel brought in, in the past, would just schedule things without my input. So I appreciate you asking."

"What happens if you can't make it in?" he asked, curious.

"They find another vet tech or they reschedule." She grinned wickedly and then pulled out her phone. "I can do this Friday, in the morning. I don't have any grooms that day, and both my employees are here to watch the dogs I will have boarding for the weekend."

Ryker typed it into his phone. "Do you think six in the morning will be too early for Christine and Dave to bring the cats?"

"No, they'll be fine."

"You're sure?" he asked, hesitating because not too many people liked early-morning appointments.

"Christine and I are good friends. She'll be thrilled you're doing this for her. I'll text her and let her know."

"*Merci.* That's fantastic." He turned back toward his car, but then turned around and before he could stop himself from offering, he blurted out, "Do you need my help herding up the chickens? I mean, I did interrupt you."

Her blue eyes widened. "You're offering me help with my horde?"

"Don't you mean flock?" he asked, trying not to chuckle.

"Sure, I mean that's what a big group of chickens is technically called, but these chickens are a horde in every sense of the word. They're mean." Harley had put an emphasis on the word *mean.*

"Then why do you have them?" Now he was amused by this whole prospect.

She shrugged. "Well, I like them. They're dicks, but I like having them around. Plus eggs are good. So, yeah, sure, if you want to help. I need to get them into their chicken coop for the night so that they're not carried off by foxes or coyotes or whatever else wants a bloodthirsty chicken."

Ryker laughed. "This description of them is not really helping your case."

Harley grinned wide, her blue eyes twinkling in the dimming light. "No, but I want to be transparent."

"Fair enough." Ryker followed her and climbed precariously over the fence.

A couple of the chickens stopped pecking to watch him warily. He noticed that there were three roosters. Which was unusual.

"Watch out for Cluck Norris Jr. He kicks a mean...kick," she warned as she walked toward the far edge of the flock.

"Which one is—" A shock wave of pain went up his shin, and he spun around to see a rooster clawing, scratching and flapping his wings. *"Merde!"*

Harley was laughing to herself. "See, Cluck Norris Jr. Aptly named because of his high kicks."

"Why junior?" he asked.

"He has an uncle out east called Cluck Norris. So I had to name him after his uncle."

"And the other two roosters?" he asked, taking a step back before Cluck Norris Jr. could line himself up and plant another kick to his already bruised leg.

"Count Cluckula is that fancy rooster. Actually he's an Appenzeller Spitzhauben, which is incredibly rare here in Canada."

"A what?" Ryker asked, as he looked at Count Cluckula who was a white-and-black-speckled rooster with a high coif of beautiful speckled caramel feathers, almost like a pompadour on top. It was very fancy indeed.

"It's a Swiss breed, but I figure Switzerland is famous for chocolate." Harley dived for a couple of hens and got them headed up the ramp. "And it's near Transylvania…sort of. Anyways, he's really no threat. He just likes the ladies."

Ryker chuckled to himself as he herded Count Cluckula into the chicken coop. "And the final rooster?"

"Wyatt Chirp, because he doesn't crow. He just chirps," Harley stated as they were herding the last of her horde into the coop.

"He chirps? Is he injured?"

"No, but Cluck Norris is a jerk and every time Wyatt would crow he'd get a kick and a peck. So, now he chirps and mostly keeps the peace among the hens."

Wyatt let out a pathetic half crow, half chirp before flapping his feathers and heading inside.

"There," Ryker proclaimed triumphantly. "They're all in."

Just as the words came out of his mouth there was a fluttering of feathers and then he felt a sharp jab to the back of his knee, a peck, and he fell down, straight into a pile of chicken excrement.

Why did this have to happen again?

A string of expletives left his mouth, and then he regretted using such strong language. It had been some time since he really cursed like that. He couldn't cuss around Justin, though there were times when he felt like it.

Harley grabbed Cluck Norris Jr. "One day, my friend, we'll make sure you're fried Texas style."

She tossed the rooster into the chicken coop where he flapped his wings to a gentle landing. He looked back at them and made eye contact with Ryker before Harley locked the chickens in their coop for the night.

"That bird," he mumbled.

Harley was grinning, her eyes twinkling as she held out her hand. "Come on, you can clean up in my place and I'll make you a tea. I'm sorry you've fallen twice at my place into a pile of poop in less than twenty-four hours."

"Yes. It seems like a coincidence."

Or a curse.

Harley chuckled. "Come on, let me help you up."

Ryker took her hand and she pulled him up. They

were standing so close, he could see the top of her head, just below his chin, and he could smell the clean scent of her shampoo. It smelled like melons and something else.

It reminded him of summer.

His pulse was pounding between his ears and he was fighting that overwhelming urge to kiss her in the middle of this chicken yard. It almost could've been considered a romantic moment, if he wasn't covered in chicken crap.

What're you doing?

This was not keeping it professional. Far from it. Instead, he took a step back.

"I don't think you want me in your house," he said. "I'm disgusting."

"And I don't think you'll want to sit in that nice luxury sedan of yours and have it smell like chicken crap. I can give your clothes a quick wash and dry. While you're waiting I'll scramble you eggs and you can imagine that you're eating Cluck Norris Jr. for revenge. Or I could make you some tea."

Ryker laughed. "I don't want to picture that, but tea would be great. I just had dinner, so I'll pass on revenge eggs."

Although he shouldn't go into her house, she was right. He didn't want the leather seats of his car to get ruined and have the lingering smell of barnyard in his car for days after. Then again, given how the tiny home was not that far from the chicken coop, he was probably going to smell it anyways and he would have to get on good terms with Cluck Norris Jr., Count Cluckula and the very bullied Wyatt Chirp.

Why did I invite him in?

That's what she was asking herself as she put the kettle on to boil while Ryker's pants were in the dryer. It hadn't been too bad to clean off the chicken mess, so to save time and on his insistence, Ryker hand-washed his jeans in her laundry sink and then tossed them in the dryer for a quick cycle.

Now, he was sitting at her kitchen table with a beach towel wrapped around his waist. Willow, who had already greeted him and got several pets, was now snoring away on the couch, on her back with her legs wantonly spread out. Ryker had just laughed at her and called her a little goof.

She had only been half paying attention to that because she was very well aware that he was pantsless, in her kitchen. When he had pulled up in her driveway he was dressed casually, but his jeans were pressed and obviously designer.

It was a city mouse, country mouse situation. She couldn't remember the last time she thought to iron jeans. Probably never. Actually, he was the first person she'd met who did.

She hadn't expected him to offer help with the chickens. No one ever did—at least, not more than once. No one ever offered again after Cluck Norris Jr. was done with them. She felt bad about his clothes, but it had also been quite comical.

Then she'd helped him stand up and he had been so close. She could smell his cologne. It was subtle, but she liked that spicy scent of his and she had just stood there, the pit of her stomach swirling, half expecting him to kiss her. Even though she wanted nothing romantic to do with him, she was shocked that she had wanted his kiss.

Harley had been relieved when he stepped away, breaking the spell.

At least, on her end. Because she was pretty sure that he wasn't feeling anything toward her, and why would he?

The kettle whistled and she shook away all those invading thoughts about kissing him.

"How would you like your tea?" she asked, hoping her voice didn't catch.

"Just black is fine." Ryker was flipping through one of her farmer reports.

She poured hot water over the tea bag and then brought him the mug. She wasn't going to have tea this late, because she wouldn't be able to sleep at night if she did, so instead she poured herself a glass of water and then joined him at the kitchen table.

Ryker was still engrossed in the report.

"Find anything interesting?" she asked.

"A lot, actually." He set the report aside. "I've

always been fascinated by farming. I'm sorry I helped myself. Rooting through your magazines."

"It's fine."

"Are you a farmer then too?"

"No. I don't really do farming," she said. "I rent out the fields. Someone else plants whatever they want. I do have a tractor though."

"My son would like to see that," he said, smiling.

"I can show him." And she would be glad to show Michel's grandson around.

"I don't want to disrupt your life."

She shrugged. "It's no bother. I'm close with Michel, and you're both important to him, so I'd be glad to. I used to be friends with Lexi Van Dorp, but we've drifted apart. I knew Daphne a little too, but she was older."

His expression softened, but she could see the brief flicker of pain behind his eyes. "Did you?"

"I didn't know her well, but this is a small town."

"*Oui*. It is. I'm not used to it."

"It's peaceful. Maybe it'll grow on you."

He smiled, taking a sip of his tea. "So tell me, does Michel's clinic get a lot of large animal patients?"

"Some. Blyth's vet clinic is exclusively large animal, but Michel gets some. Have you ever had to do a C-section in minus forty?"

Ryker winced. "No."

"Stick around until calving time next February and you might," she teased.

"I think that is a pleasure I will miss out on." He sighed. "In my city clinic, C-sections are done in a comfortable operating room."

And there it was. Confirmation yet again that he didn't plan on staying. She knew that it would disappoint Michel that he couldn't hand over the reins of his clinic to Ryker and properly retire. The clinic would probably close, which would be so awful for the community.

It really wasn't her business, but maybe there was some way that she could convince Ryker to stay.

And why would you want that?

Harley ignored that little voice, telling herself that it wasn't for her, but for Opulence and the animals here. Someone needed to replace Michel full-time, but would Ryker really uproot his child? Probably not.

"So have you worked with large animals?" she asked, changing the subject from him leaving at the end of summer.

"A bit. I have delivered a few cows and a horse," he admitted, finishing his tea. "What kind of animals are farmed around here?"

"Mostly chickens," she joked, picking up his empty mug and taking it to the dishwasher.

He cursed under his breath, laughing softly. "And?"

"Pigs, but they're highly regulated. You won't really see them out wallowing in the muck."

"Biohazard risks. Swine flu, *oui*?" Ryker asked.

She nodded. "So, large animal vets fully versed in biohazard safety handle those pigs. There's also some dairy and cattle."

"I like cows."

"Me too. But my 'farm' is limited to the chickens and my rescue alpacas."

"I am aware," he remarked, dryly.

Warmth bloomed in her cheeks as she thought of their first meeting in the alpaca pen. "Right." They shared a smile.

"It can't be easy to look after all those animals and run your business. You are a woman of many talents."

She could feel the heat creeping up her neck. "Thanks."

The dryer dinged. "I guess that is my cue to go."

"Right. Thanks for your help with the chickens."

"My pleasure." He bowed slightly, in an exaggerated way that made her giggle quietly.

"So what time should I expect you and your son?" she asked, following him to the dryer.

"I think after breakfast. Around eight. Thank you for renting us the tiny home. It's perfect for us." He ducked into the bathroom and came out with his pants back on and placed the towel in the hamper.

"It's no problem." She crossed her arms again, taking a step back while he slipped on his shoes and jacket. It was dark out now, and there were fireflies fluttering in the long grass next to her barn. Their little lights winking on and off.

"I'll see you tomorrow. Good night, Harley," he said quietly.

"Good night, Ryker."

He waved as he stepped outside. She closed the door and watched him climb into his car and drive out onto the lane. Willow came trotting in from the living room and sneezed. Harley turned to look at her.

"You missed him."

Willow sneezed and shook her head again.

"You'll see him tomorrow. He's our new neighbor."

Temptation was her new neighbor, and someone she was going to be working with very closely over the summer. She had to keep reminding herself that she couldn't get caught up with someone who was going to leave. She was over Jason, but was she over the hurt of having a life-changing decision made for her, all because she was happy with life in Opulence?

No.

She wouldn't do that to herself ever again.

She couldn't open her heart to a temporary resident.

CHAPTER SIX

DESPITE AVOIDING CAFFEINE before bed and even though she was bone-weary exhausted, Harley's mind refused to shut down. She just tossed and turned. It was highly frustrating. All she could think about was Ryker and how she acted like a fool around him.

At least, she felt like she acted like a fool and that made her angry. At herself. She was better than this. Yes, her tendency to ramble was quirky and overly friendly, as her friends sometimes said, but she was usually able to keep it professional. It was only when Ryker was around that she felt kind of giddy and nervous and lost control completely.

Almost like she had a crush.

The last thing she wanted. There was no way she was going to let that happen again. She was way more guarded now. More protected.

More alone.

Yeah. There was no denying that. She had her animals, but no one to share her life with. This business had always been her end game, but part of that dream was also to have a loving partner, kids.

That was something she had mourned when Jason shattered her heart.

Even though she repeated the mantra in her head, all night, that Ryker was off-limits, she still couldn't sleep. Not well, anyway. Eventually, annoyed with her non-sleeping, Willow got up, heaved a huge sigh of disdain and left the bedroom for the couch downstairs.

When Harley got up that morning to do her rounds, she headed straight for the coffee and received some serious side-eye from Willow, who was looking at her with extreme accusation that she had interrupted her good night's sleep in the cushy bed.

"Sorry," Harley muttered to Willow as the dog trotted ahead of her outside so that she could relieve herself.

Usually, Willow would come to the barn to check on the alpacas and dogs, if they were boarding any, which they weren't at the moment, but after Willow did what she needed to do, she headed back to the mudroom door where Harley let her in.

"Traitor," Harley grumbled, as Willow slipped past her back into the house and headed straight for her comfy spot in the living room.

Harley was slightly envious because she would love to have a nap right about now, but the animals always came first and it was almost nine in the morning. The alpacas would be wondering where she was, and the chickens would have to be let out soon.

She dragged herself slowly across her driveway when she heard the sound of wheels on the gravel lane. Her heart did a little pitter-patter in the pit of her stomach as she recognized the dark sedan with the Quebec license plates.

Why is he here so early?

And then she remembered it was move-in day, and it wasn't that early. She was just late with her chores. He had even told her he'd be there early. What she needed to do right now was pull herself together.

Ryker slowed and rolled down his tinted window, and she tried to stifle a nervous yawn.

"Good morning," he said brightly, his gray eyes twinkling. "How are you?"

"Good." She was lying. She was exhausted. "How is your leg?"

"My leg?" he asked.

"From your attack last night," she teased.

"He has a big bruise!" A little voice spoke up from the back.

Ryker groaned and then rolled down the window in the back seat next to him. A little boy with reddish hair and big green eyes stared up at her. It took her breath away for a moment, because she saw Michel's eyes—Daphne's eyes—staring back at her.

"You must be Justin," Harley said, fighting the overwhelming emotions bubbling up inside her.

He looked so much like his mom.

"Yep," Justin responded.

"Justin, this is Harley Bedard." Harley waved as Ryker introduced her. "She's our landlord, and she owns this farm."

"Can I see the attack chicken?"

"Later," Ryker replied patiently. "We have to move in first."

Justin looked crestfallen.

"I promise, you're here for the summer so you will meet all the chickens," Harley said, trying to ease Justin's disappointment.

Justin smiled again and pumped his fist.

Harley turned back to Ryker. "Do you need anything from me?"

"I don't think so. Oh, the water and electricity are on, yes?"

Crap.

That's what she'd forgotten to do.

"No. So let me release my alpacas, and then I'll make my way to your place and show you how to power it all up."

"Sounds good." Ryker pulled away, slowly, headed down the lane to behind the chicken house where the bright turquoise tiny home sat.

Harley quickly made her way to her livestock barn, which housed the three rescue alpacas. It was only supposed to house two of them, Vince and Zuul, but then they had Gozer and honestly for one brief moment Harley thought, given the characters they were named after, the end of the world might actually come.

It didn't, but they were dramatic nonetheless and made their displeasure about her lateness well-known. She made sure they had feed in their outside trough, and water, then she climbed into their pen and let them out into their small outside pasture.

She wasn't wearing her headphones this time, so she wouldn't be startled by anyone sneaking up behind her.

She chuckled remembering that. So humiliating. At least Ryker had a good humor about it.

Then her blood heated as she remembered him on top of her.

Those gray eyes gazing into her eyes.

Get a grip.

After she took care of Ryker's needs at the rental, she'd come and muck out their stall and put down fresh bedding for the night. Thankfully, in summertime, there wasn't a whole lot she had to do. They were very content grazing in the long grasses of her small pasture.

She was going to be very quick about getting everything at the tiny house all set up so that she could give Ryker the space he needed with this son and keep her distance from him.

For a moment she thought again that it might be nice to have a nap, but then she snorted and laughed to herself as she made her way to Ryker's place for the summer.

A nap. What's that?

Ryker had the front door open and there were a couple of suitcases still sitting on the front porch. There was also a bike leaning up against the side of the house, and Justin was bouncing a basketball on the gravel lane.

He glanced up as she came over.

"There's a basketball hoop hanging off the side of the old barn with a small concrete pad if you want to play," Harley offered.

It had been there when she bought the property. The basketball hoop didn't have a net, but she just never bothered to take it down.

"Really?" Justin asked.

Harley nodded. "You don't have to just hang out in front of this house. The only places I don't want you to go without adult supervision are the green building near the road and that fenced-in area. Oh, and the old barn has my rescue alpacas. It's best to keep away from them. Zuul is a bit protective of her baby right now."

"Dad," Justin shouted. "Can I go play basketball at the barn? Ms. Bedard said there's a hoop there."

Ryker stepped out of the house, ducking slightly. "You're okay with that? I don't want him to get in your way."

"It's fine." Which was true. Someone better get use out of the basketball hoop.

Justin looked so eager. Ryker pursed his lips together. "*D'accord*, but I want you to bring in the last of your things and set up your bed first."

Justin groaned and set his basketball down. "Fine."

Harley watched as he opened the back seat and

pulled out a knapsack and a very weathered fleece blanket. Covered with dogs.

A lump rose in her throat as she saw it.

It was the no-sew fleece blanket that she had made for Justin, or rather she had sent it to Daphne for the baby shower she couldn't attend because she had been in school. Daphne had loved it and wrote her a lovely thank-you letter. When Justin had been born, Michel had sent her a baby picture.

"Can I see that?" Harley asked.

Justin nodded and handed her the blanket. The fleece had pilled, but it was still soft and it was obviously well loved. It made her overjoyed to know that.

"It's been my blanket since I was a baby," Justin said softly.

"I know," Harley whispered.

"How do you know?" Justin asked.

She grinned and handed Justin back the blanket. "I made it for you."

Ryker wasn't sure he registered what Harley was saying at first. He had been standing there processing how happy Justin seemed to be and how well he was interacting with Harley.

Justin often struggled with new people. He shied away. The fact that he was conversing with her, especially about his blanket, gave Ryker hope, and then she said she made it.

Her expression had sobered when she saw Justin's baby blanket. Daphne had received it at her surprise baby shower. They had been in Goderich visiting her parents and there was a baby shower, with a lot of friends and family. Presents had been sent from those who couldn't make it, and Ryker distinctly remembered when Daphne had opened that blanket. She had loved it so much and the day they had brought Justin home from the hospital, he had come home in that blanket.

It was Justin's safety and security. The thing he clung to the most, besides his dad.

And Harley had made it?

The blanket that Justin clung to when he learned his mother had died. The comfort and love that had been shared with that blanket. Ryker was trying to fight back the tears that were threatening to spill, because he didn't want Justin to see him cry.

"You made this?" Justin asked excitedly. "You knew my mom?"

Harley smiled at Justin. Ryker's breath caught in his throat. Watching her with his son melted his heart. Seeing his son so engaged, like he used to be.

Don't, a little voice warned.

She was off-limits.

"I did. Though, she was older than me. We grew up in the same town. Everyone knows everyone here."

Justin looked down at his blanket lovingly. "That's so cool."

"I think so," Harley remarked and then looked

up at Ryker, and he couldn't help but smile at her tenderly. Even though he shouldn't, he couldn't help himself. It was cool, as Justin had said. Justin was so engaged. He couldn't remember the last time Justin had volunteered to play outside on his own. They'd only been here, in Opulence, a couple of days and Justin was almost back to his normal self.

He was happy.

Maybe it'll last? Maybe you can stay?

Ryker shook that thought away. There was no sense in getting ahead of himself. Better to take things one day at a time.

"Come on, Justin. Bring your stuff inside and then you can go play basketball," Ryker said, hoping his voice didn't break with all the emotions rushing around inside him.

"Right!" Justin grabbed his knapsack off the ground and tore into the house.

Ryker stepped outside and approached Harley, not sure of what to say. "I didn't know you were there at the baby shower."

"I wasn't," Harley said quickly. "I was at school, but I sent the gift. Bought the fabric from a fabric store on Queen Street, in the fabric district no less, then I put it together in my dorm room and mailed it to my mom, who took it to Michel's for the baby shower."

"Well, your present meant so much to Daphne and to Justin."

And to me.

Only he didn't say that part out loud.

"Well, I'm glad." Pink tinged her cheeks. He loved the way she blushed. It was endearing.

Enchanting.

"Right," he said hesitantly, breaking the tension that was simmering between them. "Power?"

"Yes," Harley responded. "Let me show you how to switch on the tiny home and all the buttons and stuff for the septic, water and solar panels."

"Solar panels?" Ryker asked in wonder.

"It's a tiny home," Harley teased. "Of course there's solar panels. It's a whole movement, this smaller scale living. It's environmentally friendly and green."

He chuckled. "Lead on."

Harley slipped off her rubber boots and he followed her into the house, confused about all these emotions she had stirred up in him with just a simple memory. Ryker wasn't one to believe in fate, but now he was questioning that disbelief, because it felt like something was tying him to Opulence.

To her.

Even after just a day. And he wasn't sure how he felt about that, because whether it was fate or not, he wasn't sure that this could be a forever home. Montreal was home.

Opulence wasn't.

CHAPTER SEVEN

RYKER HAD FOOLISHLY thought that Justin would want to spend the day with him. But the moment the bags were set in their respective rooms, or rather lofts, Justin grabbed his basketball and ran outside.

Ryker was pleasantly surprised. Actually, flabbergasted was a better word.

It took Justin a while to warm up to places and people now, and that was hard to watch, especially when Justin had been so adventurous before.

He thought it would take Justin longer to get settled into their new residence, because when they had been coming to Ontario to spend the summer Justin had been slightly nervous to leave Montreal.

Yet, there was a part of him that wasn't surprised by Justin taking to the tiny home on the farm property as fast as he did, because the moment they had pulled into Michel and Maureen's driveway after their eight-hour car ride, Justin was no longer nervous and had appeared to take to the idea of this summer in Huron County with gusto.

Apparently, this was no different. How could he say no when Justin eagerly asked to play basketball again?

Ryker couldn't.

It thrilled him to hear Justin's laughter again,

the excitement in his voice about where they were staying.

Justin said he loved it.

All of it.

Ryker thought it would do.

He had to sometimes duck, in the cramped space, but surprisingly it was laid out quite smartly.

There were two lofts. One of them had stairs with storage drawers under each step. The other loft, which Justin had claimed as his hideaway, had a folding ladder. Ryker was fine by that, as he preferred the stairs.

The main floor of the tiny home had a modern kitchen with an island and there was a cozy living room with a couple of chairs, a television on the wall and a small wood burning stove that Ryker doubted they would be using. Under his loft, there was a beautiful bathroom that overlooked the fields and the forest.

Outside there was a covered porch with a wraparound deck and brightly colored Muskoka chairs. When he walked around the side, he found a small propane barbecue.

It was the perfect summer hideaway.

Ryker took a seat in one of the Muskoka chairs, where he could see that Justin was making use of the basketball hoop. He could hear the rhythmic dribbling and the sound of the ball bouncing off the backboard.

It had been a long time since he heard that sound.

He closed his eyes, just listening to that sound. It was the first time in a while where Justin wasn't glued to his side, moping and fearful.

"Pappa! Look at me," Justin shouted.

Ryker cracked open an eye. "What, buddy?"

Justin did a trick shot. It bounced off the backboard and dropped in the hoop.

"See that, Pappa?" Justin exclaimed.

"C'est magnifique!"

Justin turned back to his game.

It was nice to have a moment to relax.

He could also hear the chickens, and for a moment he glared in direction of the chicken coop, knowing that Cluck Norris Jr. was there. Then he laughed as he thought of that ridiculous scene from last night, and then he thought of Harley again. Thought of her constant chatter.

Her smile.

Her laugh.

He couldn't help but wonder where she was.

He could hear some soft humming. Almost like a droning.

He got up and walked toward the old barn that had a fenced-in pasture. He could see that Harley was out there, and she was dragging a mineral lick. There were three alpacas in the grass, very interested in her and her work. The mineral lick looked heavy.

When he had startled Harley and she had pulled

him down into their pen, he hadn't noticed how many alpacas usually occupied that space.

Now, he could get a good look at them. Leaning over the fence, he watched Harley interact with them.

Two adults and one little one.

He smiled as he watched the alpacas gently nudge her. Harley then dug in the pocket of her overalls and pulled out some carrots, which they happily lapped up from the palm of her hand with their waggling lips.

She had the touch when it came to animals.

It had been really apparent to him when they had worked together in the cat rescue. He didn't have to give her much instruction. Once he had shown her how easy it was to microchip the cats, she did it like a pro.

It was like she understood exactly what he needed in each moment. He had never worked with someone like that. Usually it would take years of working together before a vet tech could anticipate what he needed, but with her in that moment at the cat rescue, it was like they were in tandem.

She looked up and saw him leaning against the picket fence. "Everything okay?"

"It is. Do you need help?" he asked.

He'd thought he'd be hunkered down with Justin all day. Now, he was unsure of what to do. Ryker had a hard time keeping still.

Harley cocked an eyebrow. "You're still dressed too nice. I will not be responsible for you falling in poop for a third time."

He laughed. "Fair enough."

She waded through the long grass toward him. "Where's your son?"

He nodded over his shoulder. "Basketball."

"Oh, good!" She crossed her arms. "I hope he likes it here."

"He seems to."

A car came roaring up the driveway; he could hear the gravel crunching.

Justin dropped his ball and came running toward him, spooked because it was someone he didn't know.

"Pappa!"

Ryker turned and walked quickly toward him. Justin cuddled up against him.

A farmer in green coveralls parked his truck. He looked like he had just come straight from the barn. There was straw all over him.

"Have you seen Harley?" the farmer asked.

"She's in the pasture." Ryker motioned over his shoulder.

"Thanks!" The farmer took off quickly, waving and calling Harley's name.

"What's wrong, Pappa?" Justin asked nervously, clutching his basketball closer.

"I don't know. Stay on the porch, *oui*?"

Justin nodded and ran toward their deck, but Ryker could tell Justin's anxiety was amped.

He made his way over to the farmer and Harley. She had her hands on her hips and was frowning, nodding.

"What's wrong?" Ryker asked.

"His cow is calving," Harley said tensely. "Or she's trying to."

Ryker was surprised. It wasn't calving season.

"I need your help, Harley. The large animal vet is on another farm. You've delivered calves before," the farmer pleaded.

"I have, but if she needs a C-section, I can't help you, Mel," Harley stated.

Mel nodded. "I know, but please come. I don't have the strength the pull the calf myself."

"Do you have a jack?" Ryker asked.

Mel nodded and then asked. "Who are you?"

Harley glanced at Ryker. "Mel, this Dr. Proulx, Michel's son-in-law. He's a vet. Can he tag along?"

Relief washed over Mel's face. "Please. Harley knows where I live. Hurry."

"Go, we'll be there," Harley reassured him.

Mel nodded and ran off to his truck.

"What about Justin?" Harley asked.

"He can come too," Ryker stated. There was no way he would be able to leave Justin alone with him so anxious, let alone leave him in a new place.

Justin often came with him to his practice when he had to work a weekend shift. Justin was not grossed out by veterinary medicine or squeamish at all.

"Do you have coveralls?" Harley asked.

"Ah, no."

"I do. Follow me."

Ryker motioned to Justin to come with them, and they followed Harley into the mudroom of her farmhouse. Willow came over and before he could say anything, boy and dog were on the floor and suddenly best friends forever. All that anxiety Justin had built up since Mel arrived seemed to melt away as his son buried his face in Willow's fur.

Harley was chuckling. "Willow loves kids."

"I can tell." A smile was tugging at the corners of his mouth as he watched his son and Harley's ridiculously tiny farm dog make friends. Willow was wagging her tail, or more to the point, her whole back end was wagging back and forth as she licked Justin's face. Justin was giggling and petting her.

"What's her name?" Justin asked.

"Willow," Harley replied as she turned to the armoire that was in her mudroom. "She seems to like you!"

"I like her!" Justin announced, his eyes shining as he petted Willow.

"So it seems," Ryker murmured.

"Can Willow come with us?" Justin asked hopefully.

"She sure can," Harley replied.

"Are you sure?" Ryker asked.

"You're bringing your kid. I'll bring mine." She winked. "It's fine."

"Yay!" Justin kissed Willow, which surprised Ryker.

Harley finished rummaging and handed him some green coveralls. "You can change in the bathroom. I have boots about your size too."

"Merci."

"I don't have boots for Justin though." Harley placed her hands on her hips, grinning as she smiled at his son and her dog.

"He won't come into the stall. He's come on calls with me and with Michel before," Ryker explained. "Besides, he has to stay with Willow, *oui*?"

Justin finally extricated himself from Willow's affection and dusted himself off. "I know what to do. I won't get messy, but I do have rubber boots at the tiny house!"

"Go get them then," Ryker said quickly.

Justin nodded and ran out the door. Willow whined, missing her new friend.

"You'll see him later," Harley replied to the dog, but Willow just sat at the back door, watching it and wagging her tail.

"I'll change." Ryker slipped into the small bathroom and quickly pulled off his nice clothes and then pulled on the one-piece coveralls. They looked like they hadn't even been used. He zipped them up.

He stepped out of the bathroom and she set a pair of rubber boots down in front of him.

"*Merci,*" he said, slipping them on. "These are new coveralls. Why haven't you worn them?"

"Uh. They weren't mine," she said quickly. "They were my ex-fiancé's. He left them with me. I should've given them away, but moved them here when I bought this place."

A flare of jealousy coursed through him. He was surprised by the green-eyed monster rearing its ugly head.

She'd been engaged?

He wondered what had happened.

It was none of his business, of course. They were friendly, but they were still strangers.

"They're nice coveralls," he said, unsure of what to say and trying to change the subject, but not doing it well.

"Exactly. Come on. We'll take my truck. I already have a bunch of vet gear packed in the lockbox."

There was no arguing with that. Justin was waiting outside, so Ryker walked out of the house, allowing Harley to lockup. This wasn't the day he planned at all, but that didn't matter.

All that mattered was getting that calf safely delivered.

Harley didn't know what came over her, mentioning who'd owned the coveralls. She'd forgotten they were even there, but as she didn't have any other coveralls to lend Ryker, there was really no choice. At least he didn't ask her questions about her ex or the fact she was engaged. Not that she had anything to hide. She just didn't want any pity from him. She didn't need that.

Justin was happily chatting about Willow and the calf that wasn't born yet as they drove the two kilometers down the road to Mel's farm. Willow was leaned up against Justin, staring up at her new buddy adoringly.

Ryker glanced over his shoulder. "I think you've been replaced in your dog's affections."

Harley peeked in her rearview mirror and giggled. "I think so."

It warmed her heart to see Justin with Willow. It was nice.

"So this is not the usual time of year for a calf," Ryker remarked.

"No. You're right. It is a bit odd to have a cow calving in the summer, but Flossie is a new heifer and Mel's bull escaped and now they're having a summer calf. Flossie is a prize dairy cow."

Ryker grinned. "An escaped bull and a prize cow. Oldest story in the book."

"Flossie is worth a lot. The calf is probably worth something too, because the bull that is Flossie's baby daddy is a prize stud as well."

"I didn't realize there was so much farmyard drama around here."

"It's a regular Days of Our Livestock here." She laughed awkwardly at her own joke, but she was the only one who did. She could almost hear crickets from the silence that descended. Even Willow cocked her head to the side in confusion.

Ryker raised his eyebrows. "What?"

"A soap opera pun." She had to stop punning all over him.

"You tell terrible jokes," Justin quipped. "I like them."

Harley and Ryker both laughed at that.

"Well, I'm glad someone does," Harley said.

They pulled into Mel's yard and parked. He was waiting for them in the barn. Flossie had been fenced off in a pen with lots of hay, and right away Harley could see that the bag that contained the calf had burst.

"It's big," Mel stated. "I've delivered calves before, but none this big."

Ryker frowned and grabbed one of the gloves that Mel handed him. A long glove that he rolled over his sleeve and up his arm.

"Hang back here, Justin, with Willow," Harley instructed as she grabbed a glove and followed Ryker into the pen. She was very familiar with Flossie, and Ryker was a city vet with less large animal experience. She didn't know if he'd understand the nuances.

It only took a minute for her to realize that Ryker knew what he was doing. He was talking calmly to Flossie as she mooed, trying so hard to deliver her calf. He gently placed his hand up inside Flossie and felt around, then removed his arm.

"Well?" Harley asked.

"I can feel the head and the legs. The calf is in position, but it's large. Quite large. I think I'll use the calf puller."

"I'll get it," Mel said. "Come on, young man, you can help me. Bring Willow too."

"Okay." Justin leaped down from where he was hanging off the fence and followed Mel. "Come on, Willow!"

"Feel," Ryker suggested to Harley.

Harley nodded and slowly approached, following Ryker and doing what she had done countless times when she helped check local cows for pregnancies. She could feel the calf there—it was alive, for now, and Ryker was not wrong. It was a large calf. Flossie's womb contracted just then and Harley slipped her hand out.

A foot came forward, but then slowly went back. It was clear that the calf was stuck.

"We're back, Pappa!" Justin called, following Mel as he brought the calf puller, sometimes called a calf jack.

"*Bonne*. Harley, hold Flossie while I get this ready."

"Right." Harley disposed of the glove and went around to Flossie's head, stroking and comforting the suffering heifer. "It'll be okay."

Ryker seemed to know exactly how to set up the jack behind Flossie. Harley always thought it looked horrible. There were metal poles, a lever and rope that went around the calf's feet. The lever cranked on a pulley, making a grinding sound. Harley preferred to tie a rope around the calf and use her body weight to help pull the calf from the heifer with each contraction, but since this calf was in distress and might die, the calf puller was needed in this instance.

Ryker readied it, pushing the handle, and there was a creaking sound. "I'll wait for another contraction."

It didn't take long. When Flossie was pushing again, Ryker used the lever, working with each contraction to carefully guide the calf out.

"I see the nose!" Justin shouted.

Harley craned her neck. Ryker was working with Flossie and once the nose had made an appearance it didn't take too long before the calf puller did its job and a calf dropped out of Flossie onto the hay bed.

Harley tied Flossie up so they could check the calf.

Ryker removed the calf puller and dropped down on his knees, rubbing the new calf with his hands vigorously. Harley joined him, their hands working together as they rubbed the newborn. Their fingers brushing. She watched him in awe, his strong hands working to keep the calf alive. There was a blink of a large brown eye and a breath.

"It's a girl," Ryker announced to Mel. "She's alive."

Harley stood up and released Flossie, who was mooing and calling to her young one. Ryker stepped back as Flossie attended to her new calf, licking and mooing to her as the large heifer calf stood up, tentatively, big eyes blinking in shock.

Harley's heart swelled with pride, seeing how much Flossie loved her little surprise calf. She met Ryker's gaze again, and his gray eyes twinkled at her. She knew he was feeling it too.

New life.

A calf that surely would've died had they not been able to come.

"This is the best part," Mel said softly. "When they love their calves so much. When they reject them, it's heartbreaking."

"No doubt," Harley agreed wistfully. "It's my favorite part too!"

"Good job, Pappa and Harley!" Justin said. "It's so cute. What're you going to call it?"

Mel scratched his head. "Don't know. Do you want to name her?"

Justin grinned. "Molly!"

"Okay. Then the calf is Molly." Mel tousled Justin's hair and then turned to Ryker. "Thank you, Dr. Proulx. You have the same love and drive as your father-in-law."

"That is a high compliment," Ryker replied, and

he smiled at her again, making her heart skip a little beat.

Ryker might not think he belonged there, but it was becoming obvious to Harley that he did.

Opulence needed him. If only he'd stay.

CHAPTER EIGHT

AFTER THE CALF had been taken care of and they checked over mama cow, they climbed back into her truck. It was well past lunchtime, and Harley's stomach was growling.

"I'm hungry, Pappa," Justin complained. Apparently Harley wasn't the only one.

"How about a burger?" Ryker teased.

Justin laughed but Harley's mouth dropped open.

"Who is telling terrible jokes now?" she asked, indignant.

"It's okay, Harley. I'm used to Pappa's bad jokes too. I wouldn't mind a hot dog though," Justin told them.

"Well, I think I have hot dogs at home," Ryker said.

Harley flicked on her blinker. "Never mind that. I know a place. It's the Freezie Witch!"

"Witches?" Justin gasped, excited.

"Witches of ice cream, hot dogs and fries," Harley announced.

"Yes! Hear that, Willow?" Justin hugged his new best friend.

Willow responded with a happy bark.

"I guess I am outvoted on going home to check for food," Ryker groused playfully. There was a secret smile hovering on his lips. "But I'm treating everyone."

"Including Willow?" Justin asked.

"Only if they have ice cream that's safe for dogs," Ryker said firmly.

"They do. They have pup cups," Harley replied. "I appreciate you offering to pay for lunch, but you don't have to."

"I insist. I greatly appreciate your rental for the summer, and it wouldn't hurt to treat my new neighbor and friend to a hot dog."

Her pulse quickened. "Friends?"

"Sure. We'll be working together. Friends is right."

They shared a smile. She liked the way he smiled at her. It made her feel warm and fuzzy. Friends wouldn't be a bad thing. It was a safer option, and Willow had already taken a shine to them.

She pulled into the parking lot of the Freezie Witch. It was a fry stand, and there was a large grassy area with picnic tables under shady trees. Harley picked the shadiest spot she could to park. She hooked Willow up to her leash while Ryker and Justin went to order.

It wasn't long before Justin came running back with a pup cup, and Ryker followed holding a box that carried three hot dogs and some bottled water.

"I got foot-longs," Ryker stated.

"They're huge!" Justin exclaimed.

"I bet!" Harley responded. Willow was slurping up her pup cup and didn't pay them any attention.

"Thanks for lunch," she said as Ryker handed her a hot dog. She grabbed a packet of mustard.

"You're thanking me again," he teased.

"I can't help it. It's a Canadian thing, right?"

He chucked softly. "I suppose it is. I do it too. Well, you're very welcome."

Justin sat out on the grass next to Willow, oblivious to their conversation.

"He seems happy here," Harley remarked.

Ryker nodded, his expression soft. "I know. It's nice to see it again."

"Again?"

Ryker sighed. "He's had some challenges. I was hoping this summer would cheer him up. It seems to be working."

"Opulence is the best. It's small, but mighty."

"It is…small." Ryker winked. "So, what about you?"

"What about me?"

"You grew up here? Have you always lived here?"

"I grew up here, but no. I haven't always lived here. I spent several years in Hamilton after college. Didn't like the city and came home."

"Did your ex move here with you?"

She choked slightly. "Wow, you're, eh?"

"Sorry."

"No, it's fine. I actually met him here. He was

a vet, with Michel. Eventually he wanted city life. I didn't. My life is here. My business is here. So, it ended."

It was one of the first times she had been so blasé about it. But Jason didn't matter, not in this moment with her new friends.

She was glad they could be friendly.

"Did he live at the farm?"

She shook her head. "No. I bought that myself. After."

"Good for you." Ryker nodded.

She released a breath she didn't know she was holding. Usually people pitied her when she told them what happened between her and Jason. They didn't care much that she had accomplished so much on her own, just that she'd been dumped. At least that was the impression she got.

Ryker just seemed impressed that she managed to buy the farm herself.

It was an accomplishment and one she was damn proud of.

They sat there, eating their hot dogs. They didn't have to say anything more.

It was just nice to sit there.

Together.

After lunch they went back to Harley's farm. Ryker went to clean up with Justin at their home, and she went back to her place to do the same.

The rest of the day, she really didn't see either of

them. Spending time with Justin and Ryker together made her feel a longing for a family. A feeling she thought she had grieved and moved on from.

You don't have time to think about this.

She had a lot of work to do at Cosmopawlitan Opulence and taking care of her animals.

Ryker had made it clear that he wanted to spend some time unpacking and getting settled into their place. When she got back from her work at the end of the day, she saw that the coveralls were cleaned, neatly folded and on the bench next to her back door.

The rest of her week was busy. She didn't have much time to spend with them, but every time she saw Ryker or Justin she'd wave or they'd exchange a few quick words.

It was nice having them around on the property.

She didn't feel so alone.

At the end of the week she'd spend time with Ryker at the vet clinic, and she was kind of looking forward to it.

When she woke up on Friday, she got ready to head into Michel's vet clinic, knowing that she would see Ryker. What she had to remind herself of was that she was there to do her work and she couldn't let all the swirling emotions interfere with that. Especially the piece of her that kind of missed him. She'd only know them for a week, and they were already weaving themselves into her life, which scared her.

It was an early start to a clinic day, as Christine was bringing in their feral cats for the barn cat program and there were a couple of friendlier cats they had to neuter, so they could be adopted. It was a full, packed day.

Ryker was an excellent vet and she knew she could work well with him, if she could keep all these ridiculous thoughts and notions out of her head for five minutes.

Harley did her chores early and greeted Kaitlyn, who was dealing with doggy day care. Then Harley went back to her house, showered and got dressed in her scrubs. She quickly braided her hair and poured her coffee into a travel mug.

It was early in the morning, but the farms that surrounded hers were already up and running. Farmers were out doing chores and doing their jobs. It was her favorite time of the day to drive down the road and into Opulence. Tractors in the fields or rumbling up dusty lanes. Shiny milk trucks speeding by her on the way to their next dairy farm.

These were the mornings she loved.

It was a short drive, but she had enough time to finish her coffee by the time she pulled into the clinic parking lot.

Ryker was already there. He was just getting out of his car when she parked her truck beside him. He was wearing dark blue scrubs and a white jacket.

It took her aback to see him in those scrubs, which seemed to bring out the color of his eyes and accented his bronzed skin.

Her heart began to beat just a bit faster.

Get control of yourself.

She climbed out of her parked vehicle. "Good morning, Dr. Proulx."

"Ryker. We're friends, remember?" he reminded her, and then smiled. "And good morning."

"Well, I figured since we're at the clinic…"

"No. It's always Ryker." They walked up the couple of steps to the front door so he could unlock it. "How are you this morning?"

"Fine," she said quickly. When really she wasn't, because she could not get him or how good he looked this morning out of her mind. It was way too early to look that good. "Where's Justin today?"

"With his grandparents. They are having another beach day and then going to London to visit his cousins. It's supposed to be hot today."

"Don't worry, the clinic is air-conditioned. We'll be as cool as cucumbers."

Stop rambling.

He nodded as he unlocked the door and punched in the security code. "I would hope so. When does the receptionist get here?"

Michel's receptionist, Sarah, had been with him a long time, and Harley was pretty sure that Sarah would be getting close to retiring soon too. Ryker would have to hire someone else to take Sarah's place.

Then she rolled her eyes. Who was she kidding? Ryker wasn't staying.

"Sarah. She'll be here at nine. By then we should be done with most of the cats from Fluffypaws, and then you can see the new puppy who is booked in later today."

"Good. I'm hoping to keep busy, but also get to know everyone," he mumbled as he went through some of the files that had been left in the inbox on Sarah's desk.

"Why?" Harley asked, point-blank.

He cocked an eyebrow and looked at her. "What do you mean, why?"

"Why bother to get to know them if you don't plan on staying?"

Sure. Just railroad him with awkward questions why don't you?

He was taken aback by that and yeah, she was being harsh, but it was the truth. He had made it perfectly clear that he wasn't sure if he was staying. The lease for her tiny home was only for the summer.

"Well," he told her. "It's polite."

It wasn't a yes and it wasn't a no, but Harley was pretty sure the noncommittal answer was most likely a no. That's usually what happened, but he was right. It was polite.

"I'm sorry for the blunt questions this morning,"

she said. "I just… I love this town, the people and the animals."

His expression softened. "I know. So, why didn't you become a vet? If you were, you could take over. Michel thinks very highly of you and your work."

Now it was his turn to be blunt with her, it seemed.

"I wanted the business that I have," she stated proudly. "I wanted to work with animals. I worked for many summers, when I was a teenager, for a dog groomer, learned things from her. I loved it. I wanted a little bit more, so I went for vet tech. I paid my own way completely and came out debt free. It was always my dream to have my own land, work with animals and be my own boss. I don't regret anything about my choices, even the not becoming a doctor thing."

Ryker smiled at her, his eyes twinkling. "You should be proud of those accomplishments. I hope you know that I wasn't looking down on the fact you're a vet tech. I would be lost without my technicians."

"I know you weren't." Heat crept up her neck and bloomed in her cheeks, and she was annoyed with herself for blushing. There was a part of her that wished he would stay to take over Michel's clinic, but uprooting a child from his home seemed highly unlikely, and she didn't want to get her—or the community's—hopes up.

"By the way, thanks for cleaning the green coveralls and folding them so nicely. You didn't have to do that. I could've cleaned them. I know the tiny house only has a small washer-dryer combo."

"It's not a problem. Thank you for lending them to me." Ryker hesitated. "Sorry I pried about your ex the other day."

Her stomach knotted and plummeted to the ground. She didn't want to think about Jason, knowing she always felt unsettled when she did.

She swallowed the lump in her throat. "It's okay. I'm over it."

And then it hit her. She was.

It had hurt, she'd been crushed, but for some reason it wasn't weird talking about it with Ryker.

And the more she did, the more she noticed it didn't sting as much to think about her ex.

Ryker knew he shouldn't have asked about her ex. It was none of his business.

He'd tried to put it out of his mind for the last week, but he couldn't.

They hadn't interacted much since their lunch after the calf was born. That moment when they were sitting at a picnic table having a couple of hot dogs had felt so right. Like it was supposed to be. It felt like they had done that many times before—having lunch and chatting. She lightened the burden and all the stress he'd been carrying when she was around. He was trying to keep his distance from her. But Harley felt like his partner. His equal.

He'd only been in Opulence for a week and here he was constantly thinking about a woman, when that should be the furthest thing from his mind.

He didn't want to push Harley away or make it all awkward. He just liked being with her.

"I'm sorry," was all he managed to get out. "Again, I really didn't mean to pry."

"Don't be sorry. It's okay. It's all in the past." She was trying to sound confident, but she wasn't looking him in the eyes and her voice shook slightly.

She mustered up a brave smile and then looked back at him, but he could see the pain under the surface.

It was a different kind of pain than his, but he recognized the pain of loving and losing. He wanted to ask her more, but he didn't.

He felt bad for bringing it all up again.

"Well, we better get everything ready. Christine and Dave should be here soon."

"Right," she replied quickly, and then cleared her throat. "They'll probably come to the back entrance. I'll go see if they're here now."

"D'accord." Ryker watched her walk away. This wasn't like him. What was coming over him? All he knew was he had to pull himself together.

Her question about him staying in Opulence had been blunt, but he answered truthfully.

Montreal was home. But working with Harley and seeing Justin thrive daily was making him see Opulence differently.

Justin has been so happy here.

Which was true, but it had only been a short time. The magic of somewhere new could easily wear off, and he couldn't move his son on a whim. Would his son be happy come fall?

Ryker pushed all those thoughts to the side as he got on with his work. He still had a lot to do. The feral cats had to be put under for their general health check, their microchipping and then their neutering. The other two cats he had already microchipped and vaccinated; they just needed to be neutered.

First, he dealt with the feral cats, because they needed the most time. Everything had to be done under anesthetic. To protect himself, but also to not stress out the cats.

Neutering usually only took about fifteen minutes to half an hour, but he had a few more things to do on them.

There was no more general chitchat as he and Harley worked in tandem seeing to the cats in their care. Soon, all of the cats were in recovery, to be released back to Christine and Dave just after lunch, but there was no time to breathe because he had a new puppy wellness check.

When he had a breather, he checked his phone. There was a text from Michel. Justin was having a panic attack and needed him. Just when he thought his son was adjusting.

He sighed.

"What's wrong?" Harley asked.

"I need to leave. Justin needs me to pick him up."

"Well, it's the lunch break and the new puppy check isn't until later, so why don't you go get him and bring him here?"

"You're sure?" he asked.

"Of course," Harley replied.

"I'll be back in time for the later appointment, I swear."

Harley nodded. "You better!"

It was a warning tease, but he appreciated her nonchalance about bringing Justin to the clinic. Not everyone he'd worked with in the past had been so easygoing.

Another point in favor of Opulence.

CHAPTER NINE

IT WAS EASY to work with Ryker. He seemed to trust her to know how to do her job. Other vets who came and went through the years, ones who didn't know her, would hover over her. Even Jason, in the beginning, had done a bit of that.

Ryker seemed to trust her skill and her judgment, which made her feel good.

It was unusual for her to open up and talk about her ex, but she was glad she did. She didn't tell Ryker the whole thing, that she'd actually been jilted, but it was nice to talk to someone who hadn't been there during that time, about her feelings.

About what happened to her.

Best of all, Ryker didn't probe or pry.

She appreciated that.

When Ryker returned with Justin, she could tell the boy was upset. His eyes were puffy, like he had been crying.

"Hey," she said carefully.

"We're back," Ryker replied stiffly.

"Is everything okay?" she asked.

"We're good. Justin wanted to spend the day here. If that doesn't bother you?"

Ryker was asking again, but she got the feeling it was for the benefit of his son.

Maybe Justin needed that reassurance from her.

Harley shrugged. "Why would it bother me?"

Justin smiled then, a half smile, but he seemed to brighten with that. "It's okay if I stay?"

"Of course," Harley replied. "Who said that it wasn't?"

"I just thought…some of the techs and other staff get annoyed when Pappa brings me to the clinic in Montreal." Justin swallowed hard. It hurt her heart to see Justin so upset and anxious. It was so hard to see someone so young hurt like this. To carry such a burden.

All she wanted to do was hug Justin, but she was still mostly a stranger to him.

"I have no problem with it. You can be my assistant for the rest of the day, if you'd like?" Harley asked, hoping it would cheer him up.

"Really?" Justin grinned, his puffy eyes lighting up.

"I'm okay with that," Ryker responded. "You have to listen to what Harley says though."

"I will." Justin jumped up and down before going to drop his bag in Michel's office.

Ryker turned to her. "Thank you."

"For what?" Harley asked.

"For being so caring to my son. He…he has a hard time leaving me some days. Today was one of those days. Then he got worried because some of the staff at the clinic where I work, they're not so kind."

Harley frowned. "I'm sorry to hear that. That's

not right. Really, it'll be no trouble. There's a bunch of supplies that need to be put away, and I'm sure that Sarah wouldn't mind some help either."

Ryker smiled, relieved, and nodded. "I'm appreciative nonetheless."

She couldn't even begin to imagine the pain Ryker was feeling, and there was a part of her that wanted to shake some sense and compassion into those people who had been unnecessarily cruel to Justin. There was no need for that.

They didn't say anything else as they both went to find Justin, who was chatting away with Sarah.

"I hear we have a helper," Sarah said brightly.

"We do. He's my helper, but I guess I can lend him to you if you need him," Harley teased, winking at Justin.

"I could show him the shredder, and I do have some letters that we need to post." Sarah smiled tenderly at Justin.

"Yay!" Justin was so excited. At least someone was excited about document shredding.

"When is the new puppy coming again?" Ryker asked Sarah.

"Three," Sarah responded. "It's an urgent one. The puppy is not doing well according to the new owners."

Harley's stomach knotted. That wasn't a good sign if a puppy wasn't thriving. It either got into something it shouldn't, picked up something it wasn't vaccinated for or, well, she didn't want to think about the worst or the idea of it coming from a puppy mill.

"There was also an email from Christine at Fluffypaws to thank you, Dr. Proulx. Apparently, the domestic cats, Bonnie, Bubba, Trouble and Hims were all adopted after they were picked up," Sarah announced. "Nia is still looking for a home."

"Really?" Harley questioned. "Nia wasn't adopted yet?"

"Maybe it's a sign," Ryker teased. "I seem to recall that she liked you very much."

"I was thinking about barn cats…" Harley mused.

"You're getting a cat?" Justin asked excitedly. "Dad, if Harley doesn't get the cat, maybe we should?"

Harley grinned at Ryker who just moaned and rolled his eyes. "I'm going to get ready for the afternoon. Justin, listen to Harley and Sarah."

"Okay, Pappa." Justin saluted his dad, who in return saluted him as he disappeared into the back.

Harley was still laughing to herself.

Maybe she *should* get some barn cats. She needed to keep the alpacas safe, and the old barn was on the verge of being infested with vermin that could pass on diseases. Lady Sif, Loki, Odin and Valkyrie were all available barn cats, so if she wanted to move forward with it, she'd just have to decide which one she wanted for her barn.

"What do you want me to do first?" Justin asked her, interrupting her thoughts.

"I think you should do some shredding with Sarah," Harley suggested.

"And I think Harley is smart," Sarah quipped, standing up. "Come on, Justin. I'll take you into my office supply room."

Justin bounced after Sarah.

Harley was about to get ready for the rest of her day when she heard frantic banging on the front door. She turned around and saw a woman cradling a small brown lump in a towel. Her eyes were wide and her hair was a mess.

Harley ran to the door. "Can I help?"

"It's my puppy. She's listless. I'm so worried," the woman replied.

"Are you the wellness check for three?" Harley asked.

"No, I don't have an appointment. I just got my puppy two days ago. Her name is Brownie," the woman sobbed as Harley bent over and checked on the vitals of the chocolate-colored pup. There was a weak pulse, but the puppy was not responding. Harley's heart sank.

"You better come in." She led the frantic woman straight to the first exam room where Ryker was waiting for the next appointment.

He was typing something on his computer and he looked up at the early interruption, startled. "Harley?"

"Not our expected puppy, but this one is not doing well," Harley explained.

"Bring the puppy here." Ryker stood up and immediately was invested.

The woman laid her wee little pup on the exam table. Ryker put on gloves and a disposable surgical gown. The silence was slightly deafening as Ryker examined the puppy.

"She's dehydrated," Ryker murmured. "How old is the puppy?"

"Her papers say she's seven weeks old. I got her two days ago from Sharpe Line Farms. They're outside of Dungannon." The woman handed the papers to Ryker.

Harley's stomach knotted and she saw red. Sharpe Line Farms was a known puppy mill. She knew that Christine, Dave and a few other animal rescue places were trying to get that place shut down. The problem was that puppy mills weren't illegal in Canada.

She had no doubt that this little puppy had parvo, and those papers the woman was handing over to Ryker were forged.

Ryker frowned. "I need to run a fecal antigen test, but first things first, this puppy is severely dehydrated. You can tell by how when I squeeze her skin, it doesn't bounce back. I need to hook her up to an intravenous."

"Okay. Please, do whatever it takes to save Brownie," the woman sobbed.

Ryker smiled. "Brownie? That is a nice name for a dog. We'll do what we can. Harley will take you out to Sarah, our receptionist, and get your information sorted. I'll keep you posted."

Ryker scooped up little Brownie and Harley opened the door for him. He was taking Brownie into the back, to the hospital part of the clinic.

The woman sobbed again and Harley put her arm around her to console her. She couldn't tell the woman everything would be okay, because there was no cure for parvo. It was up to the dog to get over it. All they could do was support the puppy's body to give it a fighting chance.

Ryker was just waiting on the result. He'd hooked up Brownie to an intravenous and some antibiotics. Then he was able to collect the small sample he needed to run the antigen test. It wasn't a complicated test, and he was pretty sure that he knew what the outcome would be.

He was pretty sure it was parvo.

The vaccines that were on all the papers Brownie came with were fake. He was checking them now and each came up nil. The vet and the vet's license number were no longer in use. In fact, the vet in question had died ten years ago and his license had lapsed.

Ryker would contact the deceased vet's family. But first, he was going to contact Animal Welfare Services to send an inspector out to this Sharpe

Line Farms. There were most likely criminal charges pending for forging a deceased vet's credentials and using a lapsed license.

No doubt this puppy had no vaccinations and had parvo.

It's why he had put on gloves right away and a disposable gown. It could spread to another dog so quickly. He was actually going to change into Michel's spare scrubs before he saw other patients.

He would have to tell Harley to do the same and then have Sarah and Justin clean the door handles, the floor and anything that Brownie's owner touched.

Harley came into the back room, her arms crossed. "Sharpe Line Farms is a puppy mill."

"*Tabarnak*," he cursed. "You are sure?"

She nodded. "Positive."

His timer went off and he checked the test. There was a dot. "So is the test."

Harley cursed under her breath. "Okay. So clean everything and have other appointments pushed?"

"I checked the file on the new patient. That's a Sharpe Line Farm puppy too. I would wager same litter. I need to see that puppy, but we need to change. We can't spread this around." Ryker picked up the phone and buzzed the front. "Sarah, please cancel the later appointments. No. I still need to see that other puppy. They both came from the same place. We have a parvo outbreak in the clinic. I need to do a deep clean."

Ryker hung up the phone and then checked on Brownie. She was resting and her vitals had perked up.

"I don't have a change of clothes," Harley said, worrying her bottom lip. "I can't go back to my farm like this."

"No. You can't," Ryker agreed. "Michel has extra scrubs in his office. Take a pair and change, and then we'll put our soiled clothes in a bag and seal it. We'll wash them in the machine in the clinic, *oui*?"

Harley nodded. "Okay. I will."

Ryker watched her scurry from the room. He made sure that Brownie was okay. He set her intravenous drip and set an alarm on his phone after he had safely disposed of his used gloves and gown and sprayed his hands with antiseptic spray.

He left his phone on the desk in the hospital room and then made his way to Michel's office. Without thinking he opened the door and walked right in on Harley, standing there in a bright pink bra and matching underwear. Her cheeks went the same color as her undergarments.

All he could do was stare—it was just for a moment, but it felt like a lifetime.

"*Veuillez m'excuser*," he said, dropping his gaze and quickly shutting the door.

He was an idiot. What had he been thinking?

He had told her to go change. Of course, he didn't expect that she would change right in Michel's office. For whatever reason he thought she would grab the spare pair of scrubs and change somewhere else.

Where?

Justin came running into the back. He was wearing a disposable gown and gloves. "Pappa, the other puppy is here. Sarah let him in and took him to exam room two. The man didn't touch any doors."

Ryker cleared his throat. "*Bonne.* I will be there as soon as I can."

Harley came out of the room, not meeting his gaze, but she smiled brightly at Justin. "You look the part of a vet."

Justin nodded. "That's the plan. The other sick puppy is in exam room two."

Justin took off, back to the front to help Sarah clean.

"Well," Ryker said, clearing his throat. "I'm going to change and then we need to check out that puppy."

"Right," Harley replied. "I'm going to get some gloves and a paper gown on too."

She walked away quickly, hiking up the too large scrub pants. She tried pulling them tighter, but that just amplified her shapely rear end, of which he'd gotten an eye full in those hot pink panties.

Stop thinking about it.

The problem was, he wasn't sure that he could. It was burned into his retinas and the fact of the matter was, he kind of liked that.

It was easier to get Harley and her pink underwear out of his mind when he saw the second puppy, who did come from the same breeder with the exact same vaccinations, or rather lack thereof.

This puppy's parvo case was worse. The antigen test came back positive and Ryker, with the help of Harley, got puppy two hooked up to an IV for fluids and antibiotics. Now all they could do was wait. Which was exactly what they were doing.

And what he planned to do for the entire night.

"It's closing time," Harley reminded him gently, as she came into the treatment room.

Ryker looked up from his computer, where he'd been typing notes. "Is it?"

"I sent Sarah home ages ago. Justin and I packaged medicine and food orders. We ran a curbside pickup."

He smiled. "Where's Justin now?"

"On Michel's computer, playing games." Harley pulled up a rolling stool and sat, staring down at their two very sick patients.

"Could you do me a favor?" he asked.

"Sure."

"Can you bring Justin a change of clothes and his pillow and blanket?"

Harley's eyes widened. "You're going to stay here?"

"*Oui.* I need to watch these puppies closely. And Justin…" He hesitated. "He can't be alone. He gets severe anxiety if we're separated, because of what happened to his mother."

"Okay. I can do that."

It was a relief she had empathy for his son. Not everyone did. It didn't seem to faze her.

Her expression softened. "Was he there, when it happened?"

"When Daphne died?" he asked.

"Yes," she whispered.

Ryker nodded. "He was. I came home with Justin after grocery shopping. We found her on the floor. She was pregnant, but it turned out to be an ectopic pregnancy. Her tube ruptured and she bled out."

"I didn't know," Harley whispered. "Michel never said how she died."

Ryker swallowed the lump in his throat. He couldn't believe he was telling Harley all of this, but she was so easy to talk to and it felt good to release it all, to talk to someone.

"I just remember him screaming. He was only seven at the time." He cleared his throat. "It's why we're here. To give Justin a break from his hyper vigilance. He hasn't been a child in so long."

"Well, this is the perfect place," Harley said brightly. "My childhood in Opulence was the best."

"Daphne often said the same."

"It's true."

"Do your parents still live in Opulence?" he asked, wanting to change the subject from Daphne.

"No, they moved into Goderich. Same condo community as Michel. They do sometimes go up to the family cottage in the Inverhuron area and my older brother and his partner have a horse farm in Ripley, which is also near Inverhuron."

"Did you grow up on a farm? Is that why you wanted to buy one of your own?" he asked.

"Nope, I just always wanted to live on a farm. I bought it after..." She trailed off for a moment then squared her shoulders. "It was always my plan. I thought it was my ex's plan as well. We talked about it, but in the end it wasn't. He changed his mind. I'm very proud I was able to do this on my own."

"You should be. Your ex sounds like an *ostie de colon*."

"A what?"

"An idiot." Ryker smiled. "Look, about earlier in Michel's office..."

"Don't worry about it. It's fine," she said quickly, a pink tinge in her cheeks. He liked the bloom of pink on her cheeks, but then he immediately thought of her in her underwear.

What are you doing? Now who's the ostie de colon?

"Anyways," he said, breaking the tension. "If you could bring Justin those items."

"How about Justin crashes at my place tonight?" Harley offered.

"What?" Ryker asked, surprised.

"I'll get him a change of clothes, we'll order in pizza to eat here and then he can come hang out with Willow and me tonight while you watch the puppies and disinfect our exposed clothing."

"I doubt Justin would agree to that." He barely would agree to staying over with Michel and Maureen without Ryker.

"We can ask him," Harley suggested. "This isn't the best place for spending the night, and Willow would love to curl up beside him on the couch."

Justin hadn't spent a night apart from him since Daphne died, but Harley was right. This was a miserable place for a kid to spend the night. He was positive that Justin would say no, but he had to ask and try.

"If he's up for it, I don't see why not," Ryker agreed. "Are you sure?"

Harley nodded. "Positive, and if he really needs to see you, I'll bring him back here."

It sounded too good to be true, and it was very sweet she was offering.

"I'll go ask him. Can you watch the puppies?"

"No problem."

Ryker cleaned his hands and headed over to Michel's office just outside the treatment room. Justin was playing a card game online. He didn't look up from his game.

"Hey, buddy. Look, I have to stay here tonight. Those puppies are really sick."

Justin frowned, disappointed. "We have to stay here?"

"*Oui*. Unless… Harley has offered for you to spend the night at her house with her dog."

Ryker held his breath. He was pretty positive Justin would say no to that suggestion.

Justin paused his game. "Really?"

"Is that something you'd like?" Ryker asked cautiously.

"Yeah!" Justin exclaimed excitedly.

"Okay." Ryker was shocked, but pleased. "Well, Harley will go get you a change of clothes so you don't give Willow parvo. Before you change clothes and leave, we'll have some pizza and then you can go home with Harley."

"Sounds good." Justin nodded and turned back to his game.

Ryker left Michel's office in shock. Justin wanted to spend the night at Harley's away from him?

Maybe it was the change of scenery?

Maybe the change was a good thing?

And maybe Ryker needed a change too.

CHAPTER TEN

AFTER ALL THAT Ryker had told her about Justin, and Daphne's death, Harley was actually very shocked that Justin had agreed to come home with her. She was pleased though, because it had made her so sad to see him upset. A little kid shouldn't have to carry such a hard burden. He should be able to play and just be a kid.

Harley had been surprised at herself when she offered, as she usually didn't babysit, but she was glad Ryker felt comfortable enough to trust her with Justin's care, and she was relieved Justin trusted her enough to accept. She was glad it seemed to have cheered him up.

After she picked up pizza, they ate quickly and Justin followed her out to the parking lot.

Ryker told Justin to be good and the boy nodded before climbing into the back of Harley's truck, eager to get to her place.

He chatted happily all the way back to the farm and once they made sure they'd sanitized, Kaitlyn brought Willow out of the kennel and back to the house. From that moment it was dog and boy, best friends reunited.

Justin absolutely adored Willow and vice versa. Willow seemed to melt away Justin's anxiety.

It actually warmed her heart to see it.

They both went over to the tiny home and collected what he needed for the night and then locked it up and headed back to her house.

She wasn't used to being around kids.

She'd wanted to be a mother, but since she closed her heart to the idea of ever falling in love again, she sort of let go of the notion, the dream of having kids. When she was younger, she used to babysit, but it was a long time since she'd done that, and her brother and his partner weren't planning on having kids, just horses, so she wasn't often around children.

Now, she worried she was going to be too boring for Justin. What did kids even like nowadays? She didn't have any video games.

At least Willow seemed to occupy him, but how long would that last?

"What're we going to do now?" Justin asked, as Willow curled up beside him on the couch.

"Now?" She scratched her head.

Crap.

She didn't know, and Justin was just staring at her expectantly. Which was exactly what she was afraid of.

"Um, well, I have chores I have to do. Then I have to do one walk through the kennel to make sure the dogs that are staying over have everything they need."

"Can I help?" Justin asked.

"You want to help me with chores?" she asked, surprised.

"Yes. I love animals," Justin explained. "I want to be a vet like my pappa and Gramps."

Warmth flooded her heart. Ryker had mentioned that Justin had anxiety and grief that were holding him back, but she was starting to see glimpses of a boy who wanted more, who loved his life with his dad and grandparents. A boy who loved it here, clearly.

Maybe if Ryker sees that he'll stay?

She shook that thought away.

No one stays, a little voice reminded her. Ryker's intentions had been clear since she met him. Their time here was only for a season.

Just because Justin was happy here now didn't mean anything was going to change. It made her sad to think about the end of summer, how empty the tiny home would be with them returning to Montreal.

"So can I help?" Justin eagerly asked, breaking through her thoughts.

"Okay, but it can be messy. You can wear the coveralls your dad wore, but they'll be big."

Justin shrugged and jumped up. "It'll be fine. I brought my boots over here because I knew you would have to deal with the other animals."

Harley smiled at him warmly. "Did you? Well, you're smarter than I thought."

"I'm super smart," Justin stated proudly.

"Okay then Mr. Super Smart, let's go do chores. Willow can come too."

"Awesome."

Harley got Justin fitted out in the very large overalls, but she had a belt and some clips that helped pin it all together. She slapped a baseball cap on his head and he slipped on his boots, following in her steps as they did the last chores for the evening.

He didn't get in her way and did exactly what she told him to.

He was a big help.

Even Kaitlyn took a shine to him before she left for the night.

Willow was completely glued to Justin's side as they bedded down her alpacas, and Vince even let Justin feed him some grapes.

As for Cluck Norris Jr. and his maniacal flock, well, Justin and Willow kept back. Surprisingly the chickens were well-behaved as she bedded them down for the night. Once they were secure in the coop she had Justin help her move the pen, so the chickens would have fresh ground to scratch at and peck the next day.

The sun was starting to set as they finished up.

"Harley!" Justin exclaimed. "What's that?"

Harley looked over her shoulder and could see the bats swooping and diving after bugs. "The bats."

"I've never seen a bat before," Justin said, his mouth agape as he watched them.

Harley laughed. "It's pretty neat, right? I mean, bats can carry rabies, but they're essential to the ecosystem. They do good by keeping the mosquitoes down. Especially when mosquitoes carry diseases like West Nile."

"Gramps told me about that," Justin remarked. "It's so cool. You don't see stuff like this in the city. Or stars."

Harley craned her neck to see the first few early evening stars poking their faces out in the darkening sky.

"No, you don't," she agreed. That was why she hadn't liked the city. She needed to go to school there, and she worked there to gain experience, but she didn't like all the noise, the light pollution, the cramped spaces.

She loved this. Maybe Jason had been right. She couldn't have been happy in Toronto. It was just that he never gave her the choice. He'd made the decision to end it without her input. She was an adult; she could make her own choices.

"I don't like Montreal," Justin said offhandedly.

"Oh?" Harley asked, gently coming up beside him. "But you're from Montreal. It can't be all bad."

"I guess not, but I like it here. The animals and my family." He looked up at her. "Mom was from here."

"I know." She placed her hand on his shoulder,

giving it a squeeze. "There's no place like this and your mother did love it here, and she loved you and your father."

Justin nodded. "I miss her."

"I'm sure you do." Tears stung her eyes as she just stood there, staring up into the evening sky with Justin, watching the bats and the stars. "I'm sure she's up there, watching you."

"I feel her more here, Harley." Then Justin slipped his small hand in hers. It surprised her but made her melt inside. She squeezed his hand, letting him know she was here too and he had a life-long friend in her.

"How about we make some popcorn, build a blanket fort and watch a movie?" she asked, hoping to lighten the mood.

"Yes!" Justin said, jumping, which made Willow jump and bark despite not knowing why she was excited. "Come on, Willow!"

Harley watched as Justin raced toward her house, with Willow following close on his heels, barking and excited. Usually, after she was done her chores, she would catch up on emails and paperwork over a cup of tea.

She couldn't remember the last time she'd slowed down and enjoyed a movie.

It sounded nice.

It would be even nicer, having someone to share it with.

Don't get attached.

She had to remind herself of that. Even though Justin had said how much he liked it here, it didn't mean that Ryker was going to stay. And she already knew she'd miss them terribly when they left.

Ryker was so tired, but his exhaustion was worth it. Both of the puppies had improved dramatically over the course of the night. They just needed monitoring today in the hospital area, and then he could release the puppies back to their owners.

Michel had heard from Sarah about the parvo puppies and how Ryker had spent the night, so he came rushing over in the morning, effectively relieving Ryker for the day so he could get some sleep.

Ryker thought he would be able to come back to the clinic just before dinner to release the puppies back to their owners, but for now, he was planning to have a nap. He was pleased that there had been no calls or texts from Harley about Justin, and he couldn't help but wonder what they had got up to. It was the longest he and Justin had been apart in two years.

After he left the clinic, he swung by the local coffee drive-through and got some doughnuts and a couple of double-doubles, since he didn't know what Harley liked. Most people he knew liked the double-double version of the coffee.

When he pulled into her driveway, Harley was sitting on the porch, cross-legged on a lounge chair and reading. She was wearing yoga pants and a tank top. Her blond hair was in a braid hanging over her shoulder, and he could see hot pink on her toenails. The reminder of her love of that color sent a rush of heat through him.

"Hey," he said, hoping his voice wasn't too laced with fatigue.

She looked up and set her book down. "How are the puppies?"

"They'll live," he replied, and then he held up the cardboard tray of coffees. "I wasn't sure what you liked."

"I like coffee however I can get it."

Ryker handed her the cup and then took a seat in the lounge chair next to hers. "How did Justin do?"

"Great! He's still sleeping. I left him a note to come outside if he was looking for me. I did my chores early when Willow got up. After she did her business she joined him back in the fort."

Ryker cocked an eyebrow. "Fort?"

"Sure, a blanket fort," she said offhandedly, taking a tentative sip of her coffee. "We both slept in there. He insisted, and I have to say that I'm too old to sleep on the floor."

Ryker chuckled. *"Oui."*

She gave him serious side-eye. "What?"

"I don't mean you're old... I mean I get that feeling of..." He threw his hands up in the air. "I'm not making that sound any better."

"Nope. So I'm old, but not old?"

"*Tabarnak*," he muttered, pinching the bridge of his nose.

Harley laughed. "I'm teasing you. And hey, it's nice someone else is putting their foot in their mouth. Usually it's me."

"Fine. Still, I don't think you're old." He winked at her, relieved she wasn't offended.

"I appreciate that you don't think I'm old," she responded. "So who is watching the puppies now?"

"Michel. If they continue their improvement, then I am going to discharge them this evening. I've already spoken to both of the owners. They were ecstatic, but are terribly upset about Sharpe Line Farms."

Harley pursed her lips together. "So am I. They've been a thorn in this area's side for years. All the rescue groups are aware of them. We've called bylaw officers, police, but there are no laws against puppy mills. There are no bylaws in this county."

"Well, we have to do something," Ryker stated.

"I've talked to Christine and Dave and some friends at other animal rescue organizations. We're going to put the word out on social media. They'll shut down for a time, but they always regroup."

"I am still going to complain to the solicitor general. Puppy mills are notorious for not giving their breeding animals sufficient food or shelter. I already have copies of the fake vaccination records. They'll send an inspector out."

Harley sat upright. "Really?"

He nodded. "Have you never had this proof from them before?"

She shook her head. "No. Just rumors and run-ins, but nothing concrete."

"I'd say two puppies that should've been vaccinated from parvo that are from the same littler and bought from the same location with almost identical and meticulously copied vaccination reports, plus a fake veterinarian identification, is cause for the inspector to descend on Sharpe Line Farms."

Harley set down her coffee and threw her arms around him. It caught him off guard, but he enjoyed the embrace. Her arms around his neck, the warmth of her body pressed against his. He wanted to hold on to that feeling.

She pulled away, wiggling in her seat. "This is so great."

"I'm glad you're pleased." He stood up. "I should go check on Justin."

"Sure, head right in." She picked up her phone and was no doubt texting Christine at Fluffypaws to let her know. She was so cute when she was excited, and he couldn't help but smile when he looked at her. She was so friendly, warm and it was obvious that Justin liked her, because he hadn't called. He'd made it through the night at her house.

In a blanket fort!

Ryker walked into the living room and Willow

let out a little woof and started wagging her tail when she saw him.

"*Tout va bien, ma chérie*. I'm just here to see Justin."

Willow seemed to understand him and trotted back into the blanket fort. Ryker peered inside and smiled when he saw his son spread out across the floor. Pillows everywhere, arms akimbo, and Willow was right in the middle of it. He could see where Harley had curled up, and it was a tiny sliver of a space. Justin had taken over most of the air mattress. The fort was made out of various quilts, and there was a string of battery-operated lights strung up on the chair backs.

Ryker shook his son gently. "Justin, I'm here."

Justin groaned and opened his eyes slowly. "Pappa? Did the puppies live?"

"*Oui*. Your gramps is there now taking care of them, but they should be able to go home later this afternoon."

Justin closed his eyes and smiled. "That's good."

"Did you have a good night?" Ryker asked.

Justin nodded. "Yes. I saw Mamma last night. It was nice. She was happy I'm here."

It felt like Ryker's heart was being squeezed. Tightly. It was hard to breathe, not in a sad way, but a good way. It was unnerving how comfortable Justin felt here and that Ryker could see glimpses of the way his son used to be, before he lost his mother.

This was what he wanted.

And he had to wonder if Justin would be okay, going back to Montreal and their life.

Why do you have to go back?

Instantly he thought of Harley, of not having to say goodbye to her, and it was a tempting thought indeed, but there was no way that he could open his heart again. If he let someone else in, if he ever entertained the idea of falling in love and having Justin love that woman too and something happened to her, well, he wasn't sure that he could survive it.

Or that Justin could.

It was just easier to be alone, and he could put distance between Harley and himself by returning to Montreal at the end of the summer. All he could allow her to be was a coworker and a friend.

That's it.

So he would have to be careful with Harley and Justin, because he didn't want Justin to get too attached to something temporary.

Why does it have to be temporary?

Justin was clearly happy here. Maybe moving to Opulence would be the best thing for him.

For the both of them?

It was a big decision, and Ryker wasn't quite sure what to do.

"I'll be outside." Ryker slowly backed out of the

tent and then headed back outside. Harley was on the phone, talking to someone, and she just gave him an enthusiastic thumbs-up, which he returned.

He couldn't allow his heart to melt around her. He couldn't allow someone else in.

Or could he?

CHAPTER ELEVEN

After Ryker had a nap, he woke up to the sounds of laughter and shouting.

Where am I?

It took him a moment for his eyes to adjust and to remember that he was not still at the clinic and that he made it back to Harley's farm. He grabbed his phone and saw the time.

Tabarnak.

He had slept for four hours and it was the afternoon. He didn't mean to sleep for that long, but he had been up all night taking care of those puppies.

Knowing Justin had been okay with Harley overnight had relaxed him. When his head hit the pillow, he was out cold.

He groaned, only because he hadn't intended to sleep so long, but also he hadn't slept that soundly in some time.

Quickly he checked his messages. Michel had texted that puppies were doing really well, which was good. It meant they could go home, but they would still need regular checkups and care. He had to clean up a bit, make arrangements with the owners and head over to the clinic to release the puppies.

He got out of bed and made his way to the window to look outside. Justin was running barefoot across the lawn with a water gun, and behind him was Harley with a seemingly never-ending hose. She looked soaked to the bone and was laughing. And he chuckled softly, watching the two of them, hearing them laugh. It had been a long time since he heard Justin giggle and shriek like that. Also, he couldn't help but wonder where the water gun came from.

It made his heart happy seeing Justin having fun, playing. Justin was at ease with Harley, which was great to see, but it was worrying too. Harley lived here and they lived in Montreal. What would happen when they left? He didn't want Justin to be hurt or get attached to something temporary.

Ryker didn't want to hurt Harley either. She deserved lasting love and happiness.

So do you.

Ryker shook that thought away. Maybe he needed happiness, but he couldn't take a chance on a possibility. Not with his son involved.

Yet watching the two of them made him long for this moment, and he thought briefly about what it would be like if things were different. If he took a chance and stayed. Except he was too afraid to take that risk.

He splashed some water on his face and headed outside, where Justin raced by him.

"Hi, Pappa!" Justin shouted, dashing around the corner of the tiny house.

"Justin..." Ryker screeched as he was blasted

with a stream of ice-cold water. He sucked in a deep breath, gasping in shock. He'd thought about having a shower, but not one on his porch, in his clothes. Definitely not a frigid cold one.

"Got ya!" Harley shouted, jumping out from behind a shrub, holding her hose. "Oh crud! Sorry!"

She turned off the nozzle.

Ryker ran his hand through his wet hair. "Well, I'm awake now."

"I'm so sorry," Harley said. "We were having a water fight."

"I figured." He walked inside and grabbed a towel before heading back outside to drip-dry. He saw Harley whispering to Justin and both of them laughing as they glanced his way.

"Pappa, you got hosed!" Justin giggled.

Harley was stifling laughter behind her hand.

He cocked an eyebrow. "I'm aware."

Justin ran off and Willow flew past the house, chasing his son with a happy bark.

"I'm so sorry." Harley apologized again, trying to hold back the laughter.

"Somehow I don't think you are," he groused, but then grinned because it was funny. Even if he was the victim.

"I truly am."

He cocked an eyebrow and she was still laughing. "Really. You seem so contrite."

"Okay. It was funny," she admitted. "Still, I'm sorry. You were not my intended target."

"It's no problem." And it wasn't. It was worth it to hear his son's happy shrieks.

"Have you heard about the puppies' status?" she asked, changing the subject.

"Yes. I'm going to go discharge them." He checked his watch. "In about an hour."

"I'm glad to hear it. At least you've had your daily shower." Her eyes were sparkling with humor. She was teasing him.

"Yeah. I appreciate that." He pulled off his wet T-shirt, not even thinking about the fact that Harley was standing right there. When he remembered, he looked up and she was looking away, her cheeks flushed. He liked that he made her blush, that she noticed him. It excited him.

Don't think like that.

He wrapped the towel around him.

"Well, I'm going to get changed, and then when I get back we'll have a barbecue. I would like to make you dinner to thank you for taking care of Justin."

"You don't have to," she said quickly.

"I want to."

It was the least he could do.

"Okay. That sounds good."

"Bonne."

She was beaming, her blue eyes twinkling. She brushed some damp hair out of her face, and he noticed tiny rivulets of water trickling over her sun-kissed skin. He resisted the urge to reach out and run his hands over her bare arms.

Both of them were dripping wet and leaving huge puddles on the deck. There was a part of him that wished he could get involved in the water fight, but he had to go change and discharge those puppies.

"Well, I better go change," he announced, clearing his throat.

"Right." She stepped off his deck. "See you later. I promise you I won't hose you again."

"I would appreciate that."

Harley turned and slowly wound the hose around her arm, heading back to her house.

If it wasn't for the puppies, he'd join in on the fun. It was nice to play again, and he was looking forward to the barbecue tonight.

But he needed some space from Harley right now. He didn't know how, but she was weaving herself into his heart, into his life.

A temporary life that could only last the summer. *Who says?*

He was beginning to think his inner voice was right.

Harley eventually managed to dry off and got Justin to change out of his wet clothes. When Ryker came back from discharging the puppies, she finished off her daily chores and changed for the barbecue. She put on a nice flowy top and leggings and braided her hair.

When she made her way back to Ryker's, she could smell the steaks and hot dogs sizzling on the grill. She had whipped up a garden salad.

Justin was setting the table that he had pulled outside. The outdoor deck lights were on, and there was a cooler full of ice and pop. Willow let out an excited bark and ran ahead of Harley to greet Justin.

"Hey, Harley!" Justin called, waving.

Ryker peeked around the corner from where he was grilling, waved and went back to the barbecue.

"I brought salad," she announced.

Justin took the bowl. "I'll put it in the fridge. Come on, Willow!"

The little dog followed Justin inside. Harley made her way around the house to speak to Ryker. Although she was feeling a bit shy. She couldn't get that image of him shirtless out of her head. It made her body heat thinking of his muscular chest and those rivulets of water running down his tanned, taut skin.

Get a grip.

Her cheeks were flushing again. She had to stop thinking about him like that. The problem was, she couldn't, and her body betrayed her every time with all the blushing.

"How did the discharges go?" she asked, trying to distract herself with work talk and hoping it would do the trick. She actually enjoyed talking about work with him. They could talk about anything, easily. It was what she liked about their conversations.

"Excellent. I think both puppies will recover." Ryker smiled, flipping a steak.

"That's great." And it was. Now if only the animal welfare inspectors would do their job and shut Sharpe Line Farms down. It was government, though, and they'd take their time.

"I want to thank you again for taking care of Justin. He had a great time. It's been ages since I've seen him this happy."

"My pleasure. He's a great kid," she said.

Which was true. She loved being around him. It was almost like they were this little family. It felt right, which was preposterous because she knew it couldn't last.

Even if she wanted it to.

Her life was here, and theirs was not.

"I've been meaning to ask," Ryker said. "Where did Justin get that water gun?"

"Ah, when we went out for lunch while you were napping. I'm sorry. It was in a discount store and I was impulsive. I'm sorry if I overstepped any boundaries buying him a water gun. He didn't ask for it, not with words."

Ryker chuckled. "It's fine. He really likes you."

Harley smiled. "I like him too."

"You should've bought yourself one," he remarked.

"The hose is so much more powerful to soak someone with."

"I remember," he groused.

"So steaks and tube steaks, eh?" she teased.

"Tube...what?" Ryker asked, horrified.

"Hot dogs." Harley pointed.

"Wieners." Ryker winked.

"Oh no," she chortled. "Why do we seem to have these odd conversations?"

He shrugged. "I don't know, but they're fun, *oui?*"

"*Oui!*" she agreed, winking at him. "You're easy to talk to."

She hadn't meant to admit that to him, but it was true.

"Am I?" he asked, his voice husky.

"Yes," she whispered. All of it was the truth; she liked being around him. "You're a good friend."

Ryker took a step toward her and took her hand in his, pulling her away from the barbecue to a more secluded spot. His strong hand, holding hers, made her heart flutter. Her body tingled and he took another step closer to her.

"It means so much," he whispered. "To have you as a friend too."

"I am glad to be your...friend," she responded breathlessly. Her stomach twisting, she trembled at the thought of him so close. She could smell him. Right now, in this moment, she wanted to be more than just friends.

She gazed into his gray eyes, falling under his spell again. She usually was so strong, but he made her melt. Before she knew what was happening his thumb brushed across her cheek, making her knees weak.

"*J'ai des sentiments pour toi. Je veux te serrer contre toi*," he said softly.

And she really regretted not remembering her high school French classes because she had no idea what he was saying, but frankly she didn't care. She couldn't help herself. She was melting in his arms and then under his lips in a kiss that wrapped her up in a hot, longing, embrace. It took her breath away. His hands ran down her back, pulling her closer to the hard planes of his body.

She just wanted to stay here forever, in this moment.

"Pappa, your meat is on fire!" Justin shouted from across the yard.

They broke apart.

Quickly.

Ryker glanced at the barbecue, which was smoking. *"Maudit!"*

Ryker opened the lid and let out the smoke while Harley stifled a nervous giggle.

"Is it…is your meat burned?" she teased, grinning and trying not to laugh.

"You have no idea." He grinned. "It's fiery."

"Right," she said breathlessly. Just as that kiss was. It had been amazing.

She'd completely lost herself in that moment when they had connected.

Why did you let that happen?

She'd wanted it to happen, but she couldn't remember who had stepped closer and who was the first to initiate the kiss. His simple touch on her sent shivers of anticipation through her whole body.

That, she remembered.

She had completely lost herself, when she shouldn't have.

They were friends.

Except friends usually didn't share passionate kisses...

"Harley," he said, his voice low. "I'm sorry if I overstepped."

"No. There's no need to apologize," she reassured him.

Justin came running up to them and their conversation ended.

"We'll talk later," he whispered, motioning his head toward Justin.

Harley nodded. Her body still thrummed with unquenched need, all for Ryker, but she couldn't let that happen again. She couldn't put her heart at risk again. It had hurt too much before. She didn't want to hurt Justin if things didn't work out, and with Ryker only here for the summer, that was inevitable.

She'd rather it be her who lost out over Ryker than his son being hurt.

It wasn't just her fragile heart on the line. There was too much at risk to even contemplate taking a chance, even a chance she wanted so very much.

A couple of weeks went by and Ryker barely saw Harley other than in passing, but they always made time to have a barbecue on Friday night, at Justin's insistence.

Truth be told, Ryker looked forward to them as well.

They hadn't talked about their kiss, but maybe it was better this way.

They worked well together and he had a better experience on the days she could assist him, but she'd been so busy with grooming appointments at her farm recently that they'd barely had a chance to work together, which was why he was looking forward to today.

He was scheduled to see Michel's regular patients, and Harley was scheduled to help all day. Michel was originally supposed to work, but Ryker had volunteered to step in while Michel and Maureen took Justin to visit his cousins in London. The clients were expecting to see Michel, but he would ease their minds.

He took a deep breath as Harley brought in the first patient.

"Sylvie, this is Dr. Proulx and he's filling in for Michel today. Dr. Proulx, this is Sylvie and her cat Bootzie."

Sylvie smiled and set her cat carrier on the exam table. Bootzie meowed from inside.

"It's nice to meet you, Dr. Proulx," Sylvie said as she opened the door to the cat carrier and Bootzie came out, flicking her black tail back and forth.

"A pleasure," Ryker said. "What brings Bootzie in today?"

"I collected a urine sample," Sylvie said, producing a bottle. "Dr. Michel gave me some beads. Bootzie has been emptying her water bowl and drinking so much. I was little worried."

"I'll take that," Harley said, taking the sample bottle away. "Standard tests, Dr. Proulx?"

"*Oui. Merci*, Harley." Ryker examined Bootzie while Harley left the exam room to test Bootzie's urine for an infection or possibly feline diabetes. He stroked the cat, who was quite content, and checked the extra skin on the cat's neck to see if there was a sign of dehydration, which could mean that there was a blockage.

"Has Bootzie been crying while trying to relieve herself?" Ryker asked, making notes.

"No. No crying," Sylvie answered. "She's been licking herself quite often and goes to the litter box more than she should, because of the water drinking."

Ryker produced a small cat treat, and Bootzie took it willingly. He smiled and petted her. "She really is a quiet, calm cat."

Sylvie smiled. "She is."

"Well, let's weigh her." Ryker picked up Bootzie and set her on the scale. She was ten pounds, which was a healthy size for a domestic cat. When he made a note of her size in her file, he could see that Bootzie was right on track.

Harley knocked and entered the room. "Her urine is testing positive for a UTI. Just. So Sylvie may have caught it early."

Ryker nodded. "I'm going to prescribe her an antibiotic, but I am still going to send Bootzie's urine for a culture and sensitivity test."

Sylvie looked concerned and looked immediately to Harley. "Should I be worried?"

"No, Dr. Proulx just needs to know what kind of bacteria is causing the UTI," Harley responded, stroking Bootzie, who purred.

"*Oui.* We're going to give her a script for a UTI, but if it's not just the general Escherichia coli, I'll need to prescribe something to kill that specific bacteria. In the meantime, the general antibiotics will give some relief to Bootzie, and I will also prescribe a painkiller to relax her when she does go to the litter box. Once I have the results, I will call you and we'll go from there. If the symptoms persist, call me." Ryker handed Sylvie the scripts, because they didn't have that particular med in the clinic. He knew she'd be able to fill it out at the local pharmacy.

"Thank you, Dr. Proulx." Sylvie smiled.

"You're most welcome." He picked up the chart

and exited the room so that Sylvie could pack up Bootzie and leave.

He made his way to the next exam room and entered it, while Harley went to retrieve his next patient.

Harley opened the other door, which led to the waiting room, and Ryker took a step back as a beagle with a small black chihuahua riding it came into the room, followed by an elderly gentleman with a cane.

"Uh, who do we have here?" Ryker asked.

Harley's eyes were twinkling. "This is Snoopy and Pepper. Best friends forever and this is their owner, Al."

"How are you today, Al?" Ryker asked, trying not to stare at the dogs. Snoopy sat down and Pepper jumped down, sitting right next to her bestie.

"Oh, terrible," Al stated.

Ryker widened his eyes, and Harley laughed quietly behind her hand. "Really?"

"Just ignore him. Al always says that. Right, Al?" Harley chided.

"I'm afraid so." Al grinned and sat down, resting his hands on his cane. "Harley knows me. She watches my other little dog, Gordo."

"You have three dogs?"

Al nodded. "My wife and I do. Donna is at home with Gordo."

"So what can I do for Pepper and Snoopy?"

Ryker asked as Harley scooped up Pepper and plopped her on the table.

"Rabies vaccines today. Gordo already had his. He's a bit of a diva, so I bring him on his own. Snoopy and Pepper, they're buddies, so they come together," Al explained.

"Very well. Harley, would you weigh Snoopy and get the vaccines ready while I examine Pepper?"

"Sure thing, Dr. Proulx." Harley made a small whistle and Snoopy followed her out into the hallway where a large scale was. Pepper whined and watched her bestie leave.

"It's okay, Peppercorn Doggy. Snoops will be back," Al reassured the little chihuahua.

Harley returned with Snoopy. "Snoopy is twenty-three pounds."

"Perfect," Ryker said. He weighed Pepper and she came in at ten pounds, which was slightly overweight for her size, but it wasn't too much. Harley was right beside him as they examined the dynamic duo.

He was very aware of how close she was and how he didn't have to give her a lot of instructions. He could smell her clean scent. His blood heated. He liked being close to her, working alongside her.

All he could think of was the night of their first barbecue. The softness of her skin, her smile, her laugh. When he held her close, she trembled under his touch.

Great.

Now he couldn't stop thinking about her lips and how he wanted to kiss her again and again.

For a moment he entertained the notion of staying in Opulence. What if he and Justin moved?

He could run this clinic with Harley by his side. Maybe they could finally talk about that kiss—and whether she wanted to kiss him again as much as he wanted to kiss her.

It caught him off guard imagining that. It was nice to daydream again.

He couldn't help but smile as he watched her with Snoopy and Pepper. Everything she did seemed to make him smile these days. It was her gentle touch with all the animals, and how she was so kind to his son.

She was just a wonderful human being, and these feelings that were hitting him were not as unwelcome as he would have thought, but no matter how much he wanted to explore them, he couldn't. He wouldn't hurt her, because there was one thing he was certain about.

He was never going to fall in love again.

That was off the table.

Is it?

CHAPTER TWELVE

WHEN THEY SAW their last patient for the day, Harley's feet were aching.

Although her days were usually packed full, she'd forgotten what a busy day at the vet clinic was like.

So even though her feet were throbbing and she could use a big glass of wine, it was still worth it for a job well done. Kaitlyn messaged to say that she had done the chores, including dealing with Cluck Norris Jr. and his mob of chickens, for which Harley was eternally grateful. All she had to do when she got home was make something for dinner, put her feet up and relax. She let out a sigh of relief she didn't even know she'd been holding.

Thankfully, it hadn't been awkward not talking about the kiss with Ryker, but it still ran through her mind all day. She just had to keep her distance, which was hard to do when they had a barbecue for the last couple of weeks, but she wouldn't trade those moments for anything.

When Justin was around, it was easier to resist temptation.

"You're still here?" Ryker asked, clearly surprised at coming outside to see her in the parking lot.

"Yes, I just had some stuff to put away." Harley stretched her shoulder, which was a bit stiff.

"Justin's with his cousins, so I was about to go to the local brewery and grab something to eat. Would you care to join me for dinner?"

Say no. Say no.

That was her first instinct, but she wouldn't mind clearing the air about their kiss. Rip the bandage off and get it over with.

"Uh, sure," she blurted out, because she felt like she was taking too long to answer him. She groaned inwardly at her own weirdness striking yet again.

This was a no-brainer. They were friends. He was her colleague and neighbor.

A tempting, gorgeous one at that, but still she could keep her cool. It was a simple meal.

Ryker nodded, pleased. "Good. I'll meet you over there?"

"Okay." She swallowed past the lump that formed in her throat. Her heart was racing, more like hammering in her chest. "See you in a few."

Ryker nodded again and climbed into his car.

She looked down at her scrubs and wished she had time to change.

Which was silly. She'd gone out to dinner with colleagues in scrubs before and it had never bothered her, until now.

Don't overthink it.

This was just a casual dinner. Nothing more.

A kiss hadn't changed anything.

Hadn't it?

She got into her truck and followed Ryker just outside of Opulence to where the small microbrewery was located. It was a popular place to grab some beer and order a casual dinner. She wondered if they would even get a table tonight as it was Friday, and this was a favorite stop in the summer with all the tourists.

Ryker was waiting for her outside the brewery. At least she wasn't the only one in scrubs. Thankfully the restaurant didn't look too busy either.

He waved as she pulled up and parked.

This shouldn't be a big deal.

So why was she so nervous?

You know why.

Because she liked being around him. She enjoyed his company. There was nothing wrong with that.

Harley ignored the sarcastic voice in her head as she climbed out of her truck.

"Do you think we'll be able to get a table?"

"I think so. I was thinking about the patio, to watch the famous Huron County sunset. Does that sound good?" he asked.

"Yes. I think that sounds nice."

"Good."

They fell into step and said nothing. Awkward was all she felt in that moment, because she wasn't sure what to say to him. Which was absolutely silly because they had chatted and worked all day. It was a good day. Long, but excellent. Right now she felt like that shy girl that she'd been when she was very young. It wasn't until she went to college that she found her own voice, her own particular brand of sass.

The kind of gumption that could Krav Maga a guy into a pile of alpaca poo.

She chuckled to herself thinking of that absurd first meeting.

"What's so funny?" he asked quizzically.

"Nothing." She didn't want to bring that incident up again. Especially how he had landed on top of her and between her legs. Heat flushed through her body, and she rubbed the back of her neck anxiously.

"Why is it suddenly so hard to talk normally?"

Ryker's eyes widened. "Is it difficult?"

"I don't know what to talk about. Except work. We could talk about that. We could discuss neutering."

Oh. My. God. Harley!

Ryker chuckled. "That's worrying."

She buried her face in her hands. "I know. I didn't actually want to talk about that."

She was absolutely mortified.

"It's okay. I've never actually discussed that at dinner."

"I'm sure you haven't. It's my brain, it's like yes, that's a good idea, let's talk about neutering and next we can talk deworming. I just tend to... I..." she stammered.

"Ramble. I know. I find it charming."

She met his gaze and his expression was soft, sincere.

Her heart fluttered. This time the flush to her cheeks wasn't embarrassment. He found her charming. "I'll take that as a compliment."

"You should."

They approached the wait-to-be-seated sign.

"Welcome!" a young girl said brightly.

"Table for two. Outside if we could?" Ryker asked the greeter.

The young girl smiled. "Of course. Right this way."

The patio was full of people, but there was a little table in the corner, with a perfect view of rolling green fields and forest. The sun was a little high still, but definitely getting ready to sink.

Ryker pulled out her seat for her. She was not used to men doing that for her. Jason never did.

As she sat down, she could feel Ryker's fingers brush the top of her shoulder, sending a tingle of pleasure down her spine.

"Thanks," she said, hoping her breath didn't catch in her throat.

"I am a gentleman at my core." He winked at her, and she couldn't help but laugh.

"I'm not used to that," she replied.

"Can I get you something to drink?" the waitress asked, interrupting them.

"Just water for me until I figure out which beer

I want," Harley responded. She'd call Brenda, the local taxi driver, to take her home if she needed it, but one beer and a good dinner of potatoes wouldn't affect her.

The waitress nodded and turned to Ryker. "And you?"

"Same," Ryker replied.

"Okay, two waters and I'll come back in a few minutes after you've checked out the menu. The special tonight is the rutabaga salad with cheese from the local goat farm."

Ryker frowned as the waitress walked away, he leaned over the table. "What is rutabaga salad?"

She laughed. "Like coleslaw, but shaved rutabaga."

"Why?" he asked, wrinkling his nose and frowning.

"It's grown around here. It's very popular, particularly around Blyth. Lots of rutabaga grown there. They have a whole festival around it. Bed races, rutabaga man…it's a thing."

"I would've never guessed." He opened his menu shaking his head. "I'm not sure I want to try it."

"It's fine. Have you never eaten rutabaga raw?" she asked.

"No!" He pulled that grossed out face again. "Is it a thing people eat?"

Harley smiled. "It is indeed. Have you ever had Huron County Fries?"

"No…" he said cautiously.

"It's fries, gravy, cheddar cheese—"

"So a poutine?" he interrupted, his mouth twitching like he was holding back a smile.

"No. Let me finish. It's fries, gravy, cheddar cheese—"

"It really sounds like a poutine." There was a twinkle in his eyes as he leaned back in his chair and crossed his arms. He was totally teasing her.

"Last time I checked a poutine didn't have cheddar cheese. It has cheese curds," she replied saucily. "You know what. You don't deserve to know what Huron County Fries are, Dr. Proulx."

They both shared a laugh.

"Go on. Tell me," Ryker urged. "Fries, gravy, cheddar cheese and…?"

"Ranch dressing, dill pickles and bacon."

Ryker made a face. "Ugh. I'd rather eat rutabaga raw."

"What do you mean 'ugh'?"

"Ranch dressing and gravy."

"Hey, cheese curds and gravy doesn't exactly sound one hundred percent appetizing either, but it's good."

"It's the best, but then Montreal has all the best food. Best bagels, best smoked meat, best poutine."

"Huron County is pretty awesome too. We have rutabaga." She laughed then and acquiesced. "Okay, Montreal is pretty good too."

"It is," he said softly.

"So about that kiss from a couple weeks ago."

There was no point in dodging the conversation any longer. She just wanted to clear the air. "I know we probably should have talked sooner, but things have been so hectic..."

"*Oui.* I'd like to talk about that as well, but I understand you've been busy."

"I'm glad we're friends."

He nodded. "Me too. I don't regret the kiss, but I would like to continue on as we have."

She sighed in relief. "So would I."

"*Très bon.*" His smile was so warm that all the awkward tension she'd been feeling melted away. For one brief moment, she wished the summer would last forever.

"Do you mind if I ask you a personal question?"

"Go ahead."

"Why are you here?" He raised his eyebrows, and she hurried to clarify. "I mean, we're lucky to have you, of course. With Michel dropping to part time and wanting to retire, we all feel that loss for our animals. He is amazing, but I have to wonder why you're here and working in the clinic for him this summer."

"It's for my son," he responded softly. "He's still grieving his mother's loss. It's hard and he's not been the same since."

"He seems like a normal kid. Worries a bit, but a great kid nonetheless."

Ryker nodded. "It's wonderful to see, but since his mother's death that normal kid has been miss-

ing. All the sports he'd play, he didn't want to any
more. He wouldn't go out to play unless I was there.
I can't be out of his eyesight. Justin gets so anxious."

"He's not here tonight," Harley said gently.

"No," Ryker replied, his voice laced in relief. "Is
it bad if I say it's nice?"

"I don't think so. You need a break too."

He nodded. "It's nice he's having fun with his
family and doesn't have to be vigilant about my
well-being. That's not something a kid should have
to worry about."

"And how about you?" she asked.

"What about me?"

"How have you been?"

Ryker wasn't sure how he was supposed to answer
that question. Was he still the same after Daphne's death? No. He was not the same man that he
had been, but he was coping. Justin couldn't even
spend the night away from him. That was before
though. Ryker was thrilled Justin had done so well
at Harley's and now this evening he was in London with relatives. It was starting to feel sort of
normal again.

Justin even had issues going to school. It was
like his son was forever on guard.

Always had to know where he was. Justin hadn't
been a kid since Daphne died.

So it was nice that Ryker had a little break because Justin was happy to be with his grandparents and cousins.

Ryker had a moment to breathe.

He was surviving, whereas Justin had not been. *Are you surviving though?*

He ignored that little thought and plastered on a fake smile. "I am fine. I am willing to be here for the summer, and see how Justin likes it. I hope our time here helps him remember how to have fun. It seems to be working."

"I hope he isn't too bored at the farm. I know I said that before, but I do worry. We're kind of isolated," Harley admitted. "My nearest neighbor is a kilometer away and their kids are teenagers. Not many kids nearby."

It was sweet that she was so concerned about his son making friends. It was on his mind too.

"He hasn't been bored," Ryker reassured her. "He loves it there. When I first told him there were dogs, alpacas and... I hesitate to use the word chickens when referring to Cluck Norris Jr., but he was very excited. He loves animals. He loves Willow."

"She loves him too. I love how much he loves animals, but we should still keep him away from Cluck Norris Jr."

Ryker pursed his lips together in a frown and rubbed the sore spot on his leg. "Yes. I still have that bruise, weeks later."

"I'm telling you, eat the farm fresh eggs and picture taking out your revenge on Cluck for every peck or scratch."

"That's kind of dark for a vet tech to say."

"What's more twisted is hanging on to him and trying to win his love."

"Can chickens love?" he wondered.

"I don't know, but I try," she said in exasperation.

"So instead of cats you'll have chickens?"

"I suppose so. Why are we talking about my chickens?" she asked, catching her breath.

"It's better than neutering!"

Harley laughed out loud. It was infectious and he couldn't help but laugh along with her. Her blue eyes were twinkling in the setting sun light. She was so charming, so personable. He could see why Michel liked her so much.

Why everyone she interacted with liked her.

It was hard not to.

It was nice just having a conversation about ridiculous chickens. It was also nice to laugh with someone his own age again. It had been some time since he'd done that, had a real conversation with someone outside of work or family. It was hard not to like Harley, to fall under her spell.

Like when he'd kissed her. He was glad she'd agreed to be friends still. Part of him really did want more, so he knew he had to be careful. A boundary of friendship would help.

"Tell me, how did you came into possession of these chickens?" he asked.

She cocked an eyebrow. "It's not that interesting. I like eggs and I thought it would make sense, so I adopted some birds. Then I had this friend who said roosters are killed almost at birth and tossed. She was running a rescue program for unwanted roosters out in Nova Scotia, which is where I was when I acquired Cluck Norris Jr., Count Cluckula and Wyatt Chirp."

"So you drove three roosters from Nova Scotia to Ontario out of sympathy?"

Harley nodded. "Yes, but they were chicks and it's not that long of a drive."

"Um, it's like twenty-some hours."

Harley shrugged. "Well, it was supposed to be my honeymoon at the time and I had all these non-refundable deposits, so Willow and I went for my honeymoon."

"Honeymoon? So how close did you get to marrying your ex?" he asked.

"Well, he left me at the altar, so pretty close."

He could hear the sadness in her voice. The hurt.

He understood pain, but his was different. Daphne hadn't run off on him, she had died, but still there was heartache there. And he could see heartbreak etched on her face and in her voice. He understood it.

Before he could stop himself, he reached across the table and took her hand in his. Her small, delicate fingers fit so nicely in his. He brushed his thumb over her knuckles and a ripple of gooseflesh broke out up her arm.

Their gazes locked and his heart was hammering as he fought the urge to pull her close and kiss those delectable, plump lips. Pink bloomed in her cheeks and her lips parted, as if she was going to say something to him.

Only she didn't. Their gazes just remained locked. His blood heated and moved through every nerve ending in his body. His pulse thumped between his ears. Her blue eyes gazed at him, full of softness.

She was beautiful. Her blond hair cascaded over her shoulders, and he wondered how soft it was. It had been some time since he'd felt stirrings of emotions, of desire, like this.

And he wasn't sure what to do.

It was nice holding her hand. Feeling that connection with someone again. Even though he should, he didn't want to let go.

"There's a fair next Friday," she said, breaking the silence.

"A fair?" he asked, curious but not letting go of her hand.

"A midway, rides and games. Maybe after we barbecue, we could take Justin?"

"That sounds like a good idea," he agreed.

"Good," she murmured, her eyes sparkling as the sun began to set. It was so hard not to kiss her again. He wanted to.

Badly.

"Ready to order?" the waitress asked, interrupting them.

Harley snatched her hand back. The pink in her cheeks turned to crimson, and she focused on the menu in front of her. Whatever moment they'd shared was gone, and it was probably for the best. "Yes, I'll have the chicken special with a salad and my French-Canadian friend here is dying to trying Huron County Fries."

There was a devilish twinkle to Harley's eyes.

Ryker just shook his head in dismay and looked at the waitress, who was smiling the widest grin he had ever seen.

"Huron County Fries! Awesome. It's just like a poutine, but with bacon!" The waitress took their menus and moved away. He cringed at the "just like poutine" comment, because it wasn't.

"Why did you order me that?" Ryker asked, trying not to laugh.

"Hey, when in Rome, eh?" She winked at him.

"Touché." He leaned back and watched the sun set over a green rolling hill. He wasn't sure what was happening with Harley, and he knew he shouldn't let anything else happen, but when he was with her it was so easy to feel like he was becoming himself again.

The man he used to know.

The fun-loving jokester and not the hollowed-out shell of a person he was now. The one he'd had to become so he could take care of his son and be there for Justin. The one who had to live day-to-day, numbly, so his son didn't have to bear the additional burden of his own grief.

The problem was, no one was there for him.

And no one ever would be, if he had his way.

What if you stayed?

The thought still scared him, but for a brief moment he let himself picture it.

He thought about leaving Montreal, of taking over Michel's practice. Working with Harley. Continuing to get to know her. It would be a risk.

And he wasn't sure he wanted to take a risk like that, at least not for himself. If they reached the end of the summer and it seemed like moving was the right decision for Justin, then he'd have to consider it. But he couldn't think about it for himself.

Not for a fleeting feeling of freedom and sharing a beautiful sunset with a gorgeous woman.

He just had to enjoy the time he had here and not muddle it up with notions of a happily-ever-after because he shared a nice moment in time with someone, because happily-ever-afters didn't exist.

He knew that loss.

He'd felt that loss.

Keenly.

CHAPTER THIRTEEN

THE REST OF the dinner they chatted about the patients they had seen throughout the day. Thankfully, they avoided all neutering chats.

She really enjoyed dinner, even though she had been having reservations about it when she drove over there. Harley had no regrets after. Except that it ended.

When they both got back to her farm, Michel brought Justin home and she said good-night instead of lingering. She had a busy weekend ahead of her and some business stuff to catch up on.

The clinic was closed on the weekend, but Ryker had his number up on the website to deal with on-call emergencies, to give Michel a break. Michel may have only dropped down to part-time hours, but he was always on call for animal emergencies. Another reason why Michel was so loved.

It was nice that Ryker was carrying on with that. Even for the short time he was here.

She had some dogs that were boarding with her over the weekend, so she was busy in her kennel and doing her chores. When she did see Ryker and Justin, it was when they were coming and going from their place. It was just a friendly wave and nothing more.

But all weekend she couldn't stop thinking about

their dinner. How Ryker had opened up about Justin and how tender he was about how she was jilted.

It was nice to have a conversation with someone who understood about pain and loss, even though they each had a different kind of loss.

It still hurt them, nonetheless. Talking about it helped.

When he reached out and took her hand, her blood heated and a rush of anticipation unfurled in the pit of her stomach. It was tender and electric at the same time.

She'd wanted to kiss him again. She'd burned with a need to press her lips against his. And the urge had surprised her.

It was a good thing the waitress interrupted them.

It had been a long time since she felt this way about someone. It was freeing, but scary because she knew that Ryker would leave after the summer.

As she moved through her hectic weekend, she found she really did miss talking to both Ryker and Justin, and for the first time in a long time, she was aware of how lonely she felt.

And she didn't like that feeling at all. It was a long, boring weekend, and although that feeling of loneliness persisted into the week, at least she had even more work to distract her. She spent some time working at the clinic with Ryker, but they were both so busy that there wasn't much time to chat, there or at home. Especially since she had clients' dogs and her own animals to care for. There was no more talk about that kiss, but there was no awkwardness either. It was like the kiss had never happened. At least, that's what she was telling herself. She couldn't get it out of her mind, but she didn't let it interfere with work, and she wasn't planning to let it interfere with their Friday plans either!

She woke up on Friday looking forward to the day and going to the fair that night.

The day dragged on, but she got her chores done early so they could head to the fair right after their dinner.

It was such a peaceful evening, with the three of them enjoying food outside and under the locust trees. The wind whispering through the boughs of spruce and the droning sounds of her alpacas out in a field. It was like the most perfect summer day.

After dinner they cleaned up and everyone piled into Ryker's car to head into Opulence for the small midway that had been set up on the fairgrounds. The sun was setting, and she could see the electric and neon lights that were lighting up the darkening sky.

"Oh, wow, look!" Justin exclaimed from the back seat. "A Ferris wheel!"

Ryker and Harley shared a smile.

"Pappa, can we go on the Ferris wheel?" Justin asked.

"Of course. We can go on all the rides," Ryker announced.

"Yes!" Justin exclaimed.

"Maybe not too many spinning ones," Harley said. "We just had dinner."

"We'll walk around first," Ryker agreed.

They found a place to park and then walked toward the ticket booth, so they could buy their passes for the rides. Justin ran ahead, and she could tell he was so excited.

"It's been a long time since I've seen him this excited. He used to get this way about Halloween or Christmas." Ryker sighed.

"This is good. He's healing."

"He is." He glanced over at her. "How long did it take you to heal from your broken heart?"

"A year." Actually, she wasn't sure it was so clear-cut. Would she ever really heal? Did a person ever really get over a blow or a loss like that? She wasn't sure. She was over Jason, but what happened was something she would always carry with her. She didn't miss him. She was just hurt by how it all ended.

She didn't like being blindsided.

"How about you?" she asked.

"I'm not really sure. I think I just focused on Justin instead of grieving, when it first happened, so it was always hanging over me. But more recently I've had time to myself and I've been feeling…

lighter. I mean, it'll always be a part of me, but…"
He trailed off.

"This is a very heavy conversation for standing in line to buy tickets," she teased gently.

"You're right. No more talk about that. Let's enjoy tonight."

"Agreed. Pinky swear?" She held out her hand, and he hooked his pinky around hers. A zing of electricity passed through her and her body heated, remembering how he kissed her, how he held her hand at the restaurant.

"Pinky swear," he replied.

They shook pinkies on it.

When they got to the ticket booth Ryker bought a whole whack of tickets, and they made their way to the rides.

It wasn't a huge midway; it was one of those traveling ones that went from community to community during the summer, but for Justin it might as well have been a big theme park, he was so excited. His eyes were twinkling and his mouth open as they walked around the grounds, scoping out where they wanted to go first. There was loud music from the games with rows and rows of brightly colored stuffed animals hanging above the booths. There were cotton candy vendors, bright shiny red candy apples and popcorn popping, making her stomach rumble with appreciation.

She couldn't remember the last time she had cotton candy.

"Pappa, they have a Haunted House! Can we go in the Haunted House?"

Ryker cocked an eyebrow. "You want to go on the Haunted House ride?"

Justin nodded. "Yes."

"Okay." Ryker made a face, and she laughed as they walked up to the false front Haunted House ride.

A little cart pulled up. Justin got in the front seat, but insisted he was brave enough to sit alone, which mean that Ryker climbed into the back seat, right up against her. They were crammed there, and he adjusted so that his arm rested on the back of the seat. She had to lean into his body, and her pulse began to quicken.

"I'll keep you safe," he teased.

"Or push me out."

The bar came down and there was a bell that rang. The cart bumped forward with a lurch and the gaudy painted Keep Out doors swung open with sounds of rattling chains. The doors shut and their cart slowly wound its way through glow-in-the-dark-painted ghosts, with a cheap piped in soundtrack of ghosts moaning, chains rattling and screams.

Justin was killing himself laughing as he looked back at them.

All Harley could focus on was the closeness of Ryker's body and how his arm made her feel so safe.

Until a plastic spider dropped down in front of

her and she screamed for a moment and then started to laugh.

"Harley, are you scared?" Justin asked.

"I hate spiders," she gasped, trying to calm her racing heart.

Justin giggled and then turned back to the ride.

"I'll keep you safe," Ryker teased, squeezing her closer.

"Thanks," she groused, but she liked the fact that he promised to keep her safe. No one had ever offered her that before, besides her parents and her older brother. She had learned to rely on herself.

No one disappointed you if you relied on yourself, but as she secretly glanced up at Ryker, she really did feel safe next to him. It felt right.

The doors opened and the dark Haunted House filled with light. The cart lurched again and came to a stop. The bar lifted and Ryker removed his arm from around her.

"What did you think of that, Justin?" Ryker asked, standing up.

"Great!" Justin exclaimed, exiting the ride.

Ryker turned to her and held out his hand. She slipped her hand in his and he helped her up. Her heart was racing and her body trembling as they stood there for a moment, before exiting the ride to join an excited Justin.

She had told herself that their kiss was a one-off. They'd both agreed that it couldn't happen again, but it was hard to remind herself of that in this moment, where they felt like a family.

After the fair they headed back to the farm. Justin had passed out, and Ryker had to carry him into their place to put him to bed. But before he had carried Justin off, he had given Harley a soft kiss on the cheek, which made her feel so warm and fuzzy, if a little confused. She had wanted more, but she knew that wasn't an option, so she did the last of her chores and sneaked off to bed herself.

She was trying not to think about how much fun she had with them, but that was impossible. Even though she was physically exhausted Harley spent another night tossing and turning, thinking about Ryker. The way he snuggled closer to her in the Haunted House and how he held her hand when they would exit the various rides together.

She loved the way he was with his son, and she loved being with them both.

It was like they were all supposed to be together.

She played out so many scenarios in her head, but always came to the same conclusion: it couldn't work. Even if Ryker were open to dating, Montreal was too far from Opulence.

When she woke up, she turned on her phone and groaned at the alerts for thunderstorms later in the day, which would be a pain to do her chores in. She saw a few missed calls pop up, but before she could register anything else the phone rang in her hand. She squinted at the screen and saw her brother's number. She knew it was her brother's by the name she assigned to it.

Dingus.

"Good morning, David," she answered, stifling a yawn.

"Harley, I need your help."

She could hear the panic in David's voice. He usually called her nerd. "What's wrong?"

"I have a foal and it's lame. Our vet is away still. Do you think you can ask Michel to come and take a look?"

"Michel is with his grandson today." She knew their schedule without needing to check.

"Damn," David cursed.

"I can see if my…" She trailed off. Ryker wasn't her anybody. "I can see if Michel's son-in-law can come. He's a vet too."

"That would be great. I'm super worried about the foal."

"No problem. If he can't come, I'll come and try to help as much as I can."

"Love you, Nerd," David said, then hung up.

Harley rolled out of bed, had a quick shower and got dressed. She finished her chores, changed out of her barn clothes and by the time she headed outside to face Ryker, Michel was there to pick up Justin.

"Morning, Michel and Justin," Harley greeted. "You got big plans for the day?"

"Morning!" Michel said. "We're taking Justin go-karting and to a museum."

Justin nodded eagerly. "Then Gramps and Nanna are coming here for dinner."

"That sounds fun. Is your dad around?"

"Yeah, he has some work so he's not going go-karting."

"We better go," Michel said, glancing over his shoulder at Justin.

The boy nodded. "Okay, Gramps. Bye, Harley!"

Harley waved as Michel and Justin drove away. She made her way over to Ryker's place. He was on the deck, his laptop open on the small bistro table, and he was sitting in a Muskoka chair.

"Morning," she said, feeling instantly nervous.

Which was silly. They'd shared an amazing kiss and nothing more. He may have kissed her softly when they got home from the fair, but it was just a friendly kiss. A peck on the cheek.

Not a burning, sensual, soul-singeing kiss like they had shared a couple of weeks ago. So she shouldn't feel so nervous around him.

"*Salut!*" he said when he saw her approaching.

"You're not interested in go-karting?" she asked.

"No. My nephews will be there, so Justin will have company. I love them, but hot sun and go-karts, no thanks."

"How about a trip to a farm outside of town to check out a lame foal?" she asked, wringing her hands, which she always did when she was nervous.

He cocked an eyebrow. "A client?"

"My brother, David, the horse breeder. His vet is away. Michel has helped out before, but I didn't want to ruin their plans."

Ryker glanced at his laptop and then closed it. *"D'accord,* but I'm supposed to cook dinner tonight for my in-laws."

"I think we'll be back by then," Harley reassured him.

"I was… I was hoping you'd come to dinner as well," he asked, his voice hopeful.

"Um…" She wanted to ask him if that was such a good idea. But Michel and Maureen were friends of hers as well, so how could she say no. "Sure."

"Parfait."

"Shall I drive?" she offered.

Ryker nodded. "Please, and in return I will not burn your dinner tonight, like Michel tends to do when he cooks."

She laughed, knowing that all too well. "Deal."

"I'll meet you by your truck in ten minutes."

Harley left. It was going to be hard to be trapped in her truck with Ryker for an hour, but she could be professional.

She had to be professional.

Just because they'd spent a cozy evening pretending to be a family at the fair didn't mean their agreement had changed. And that cheek-kiss last night had meant nothing.

She grabbed her gear and met Ryker at her truck.

He loaded her gear and his into the back of the vehicle and then climbed into the passenger seat. He looked really good in his faded denim jeans and his plaid shirt. At least he was better dressed for work at a farm. This time if he fell in poo, she wouldn't feel so bad.

She snickered at that thought.

"What?" he asked. "I got this at the tack shop. Is it wrong?"

"No. It's perfect. I was thinking about poop." She groaned as the words tumbled out of her mouth.

He snorted. "I understand what you meant. Why do you think I bought this outfit?"

"It looks great," she told him. It really did. She was trying not to stare too much.

"How far away is your brother's ranch?" he asked.

"Just over an hour. We're leaving Huron County for Bruce County." She waggled her eyebrows, trying to break the tension with some silliness as they drove away.

"Exciting for a Saturday," he responded drolly. He smiled at her warmly, and her heart skipped a beat. The feeling of his lips, the memories of their kiss and his strong arm around her at the fair last night played on an endless loop in her mind. This was going to be a long, long ride to David's ranch.

Ryker had been hoping for a quiet day to catch up on reports. He'd called to check on the parvo puppies, both back with their owners by now, and they were both doing well. He'd also formulated a letter to get someone to inspect Sharpe Line Farms' breeding facilities. He sent that off right away.

All productive busywork that didn't distract from the fact that he couldn't stop thinking about Harley. He knew they'd agreed to be just friends, and he still knew that was the smart thing to do, but other ideas kept sneaking in: that kiss. He didn't know what came over him. She was standing there and he just couldn't help himself. The kiss had been everything he thought it would be. And it had been on his mind for weeks.

Then he told her that he wanted to hold her close and kiss her in French, and he was pretty sure she didn't know what he said.

It was sweet and overwhelming. She was so soft in his arms, and he wanted so much more. He was glad when Justin had interrupted them. Or so he told himself.

He'd thought a night at the fair would distract him, but instead it drew him closer to her. It was so nice to feel normal again. Him, Harley and Justin. It was like it was meant to be.

They had chatted about how long it took to get over heartache. He wasn't sure if one ever did, rather suspecting that one learned to live with it, but there could be room for another person. Which was silly. How could he even contemplate that?

All night he couldn't stop thinking about her and

how he burned for her. She made him feel like he wanted to take a risk again, and that scared him. There was a lot to process. Part of him was saying to leave and head back to Montreal, but the summer wasn't over. Justin would be crushed if they left early. His son was so content here.

He was happy.

It felt like a heavy weight of grief was being lifted off his shoulders, and he didn't know how to process it all. Maybe it was time for a change?

He was falling for Harley and he didn't know what to do.

"Will you tell me about David's ranch?" he asked, trying not to think about her lips. He just wanted to talk about anything so he didn't have to think about how close she was to him, how he could smell her scent of melons and cucumber.

"His ranch?" she asked, not taking her eyes off the road. "Not much to tell. My brother loved racehorses so much he studied equine care and management in Ridgetown. That's where he met his partner, Armand. They fell in love and they started breeding some of the most sought-after racehorses in the county. David also has stud horses that are also in demand, and he also teaches horseback riding. Equestrian and western."

Ryker was impressed. "So he knows his horses."

"Yep. Usually if there's a horse problem, he and Armand can handle it. When he calls me or his vet for help, then it's not good. It's something completely out of his depth."

"You said the foal was lame?" Ryker asked.

She nodded. "I don't know what degree of lameness, just that David sounded really distressed when he called."

"Well, we'll see what we can do."

"I appreciate that." She glanced at him, her blue eyes full of warmth, which made him feel a rush of emotions again.

She was enchanting, and being with her made him feel alive again. He'd been living in a fog for so long, trying to be strong for Justin, it was nice to feel something. Even if it was something he shouldn't.

The rest of the ride was pretty quiet. He looked out the window, enjoying the scenery as they drove north up the Lake Huron coast. He could see windmills, farms, crops and trailers in the distance, and occasionally a tractor on the road, which slowed them up.

Finally, they turned off the main highway and down a gravel road that led to a dead end. There was a huge western-style gate at the end of the gravel road that said Bedard and Soukh Ranch, with a beautiful engraved mustang running across a field with a burning gold sunset of Lake Huron in the background.

Harley buzzed in and the gate swung open.

He raised his eyebrows, impressed.

Harley shrugged. "They do very well. They practically have their own vet clinic on-site."

"Impressive."

Harley knew exactly where she was going, and as she approached a massive, beautiful modern barn Ryker could see there were two men waiting, with a nervous foal in an outside pen, just lying in the dirt. The mother was nearby, but separated so that she wouldn't nip at them. Or at least, Ryker assumed it was the mother.

Harley parked her truck and a blond man came over, his arms wide open. "Hey, Nerd."

They climbed out of the truck and Harley gave the man who called her a nerd, a hug. "Hey, Dingus. So this is Michel's son-in-law, Ryker. Ryker, this is my brother, David Bedard, and that other man coming this way is his partner, Armand."

"Your brother-in-law," David corrected her. He turned to Ryker and the same blue eyes that Harley had shined back at him, his appreciation evident. "I am so glad you could come at such short notice."

"It is no problem," Ryker assured him, taking David's hand.

Armand came and introduced himself next and then gave Harley a big hug.

"So, tell me about this foal," Ryker said, trying to get to the business at hand. Justin was expecting him to be at home tonight and he had promised to cook Michel and Maureen dinner.

And Harley. You invited Harley as well.

The sooner he saw this foal, the better.

"Adele was born about three days ago," Armand stated. "The lameness started this morning—she won't put any weight on her leg, and you can tell she's in pain. I am worried about an infection. I have seen that before, bacteria that gets in through the umbilicus."

"You're not wrong," Ryker agreed as he made his way to the pen cautiously.

The foal in question tried to stand, but it was evident by the way she didn't put weight on that leg and the way she tried to hobble away that the leg was paining her. The foal collapsed on the ground.

She was a young foal, so if it was something infectious like infection of the bone plates or joints, then she would have a fighting chance. What he needed was a blood test, but for now he could help ease some of the pain.

"Harley mentioned you have a treatment space for your regular vet," Ryker asked. "Can we get the foal in there so I can take a look?"

"We sure do," David stated. "We have an ultrasound machine and painkillers. Everything our vet needs."

He was very impressed. They put their animals first, like any good farmer or any good breeder. He couldn't help but think of Sharpe Line Farms and how they were anything but the definition of good.

Armand and David worked to get the foal standing, and then Armand picked her up to carry her into the barn, while David calmed down the mother.

"I'll show you the way in. They have gowns and everything. Armand took some animal science courses. They are very involved with their horses and all their animals," Harley stated.

"I admire that," Ryker admitted. "To run an operation like this is impressive."

"David is a savvy businessman. I always admired him for that," Harley admitted.

What he wanted to tell her was that she was too, building a grooming and boarding facility on her own from the ground up, while also working as a vet tech. That was something to be applauded for too.

They walked through the main office, and Harley led him to the treatment room. He put on a disposable gown and gloves and then made his way into the spacious and clean room. The foal was lying there again, but then stood in the small pen with Armand soothing her.

Ryker approached Adele and spoke softly to her. He knelt down and got a look at the leg in question. There was swelling and as he gently palpated the area he knew it hurt the horse, but he didn't think it was an infection as he felt her leg and saw the trouble.

"I think it's her coffin bone," Ryker said. "I would need an X-ray to be sure."

"Coffin bone?" Armand asked. "Can that be healed in one so young?"

Ryker nodded. "It can. She'll need rest, but again I would need an X-ray. We'll still do a blood test to be sure, and I will give the foal some pain relief."

"All our meds are in that cabinet. It's unlocked," David said, coming into the treatment room. "We do have a portable X-ray machine."

"I can operate it," Harley volunteered. "Animal radiology was something of a speciality."

Ryker grinned. "*Bonne*. Then I'll give her some pain relief, give her something to calm her down and we'll X-ray her."

"It's in the next room," Armand stated.

"I'll need you to insert the plate," Harley said to Ryker. "I'll get the machine ready and pull out the lead vests."

"*Bonne.*" Ryker hadn't done many equine X-rays, but he knew how they were done. He was glad Harley was here and familiar with how the machine at her brother's farm worked. In Montreal the vet techs were the ones who ran the diagnostic machines, for the most part.

He was way more hands-on here than in the city, and he liked it. It surprised him how much.

After Ryker had done the blood work and given the foal some pain relief, Armand led her out into the next room. It was clear that the pain medicine was already helping, as well as the mild sedatives to help calm her down.

Harley helped him on with a lead vest and then helped Armand on with his while Ryker held Adele. He stroked her muzzle and told her what a good girl she was.

"The plate is on that table," Harley said, quietly before she readied the machine and slowly inched it toward Adele on its long swinging arm.

"Merci." Ryker picked up the plate on a long handle and knelt down slowly.

Armand continued to speak in soothing tones.

A red light flashed on Adele's chestnut-colored leg. She moved her sore foot once, lifting it up, but then gently put it back down and stood still.

"Ready," Harley said.

Ryker slipped the plate between the foal's legs, and Harley counted down and took the X-rays in quick succession.

"All done," she said.

Ryker removed the plate and set it down. Armand led Adele out of the X-ray room and they removed their lead vests to head back into the treatment room.

The diagnostic images had been sent to the computer in the treatment room and David was bringing the images up. Ryker went through the images.

"It is her coffin bone." Ryker pointed to where the fracture was in the front hoof. "See, the distal phalanx or coffin bone."

"At least it's not bacterial," David remarked, although he still sounded disappointed because that fracture was not an easy one to recover from, as Ryker knew firsthand.

"She is small enough and doesn't weigh too much. Adele should recover. She'll need a bar shoe, and we'll have to keep repeating X-rays until it's completely healed. It will take several months."

David nodded. "I do have bar shoes. And I have small ones."

"Well, let's get the shoe on her and then have her rest in her stall with her mother. She's been through enough stress today. Make sure you let me know about the results of the blood work, and I'll leave a note for your regular vet and where he can contact me."

David grinned and shook Ryker's hand. "Thank you again, Doc. Be sure to send me your bill."

"He will," Harley reassured her brother.

David and Armand led Adele out of the treatment room to take her to the barn where they shoed their horses. Adele was young enough that Ryker had no doubt the coffin bone would heal with rest and the help of the bar shoe, which was a circular horseshoe that joined the heel together and prevented movement of the hoof.

Ryker typed up his notes and recording the testing he did on Adele for David and Armand's vet.

"You did really good in there," Harley remarked. "For a city vet."

He smiled, pleased she was happy. "Well, I'm not used to taking X-rays of a horse in the city. It's definitely more hands-on here."

"It is, and that's what I love about it. Remember, I worked in a city too," she reminded.

"I remember you saying how much you don't like the city."

"I don't hate it, I just prefer it here."

He nodded. "I understand that."

"Can I ask you a question?"

"Of course," he replied as he continued to type in his notes.

"Why don't you own your own practice yet?" she teased.

Ryker took a deep breath. "It's been my dream. Justin was born shortly after Daphne and I married, so I was never in a rush to strike out on my own."

Another reason why taking on Michel's clinic was tempting. A practice that had everything set up? Clients, equipment, staff. It was too good to be true. Still, it was nerve-racking to think about taking it over and leaving the safety net of Montreal. Could he carry the burden of his own business on his shoulders? He wasn't sure that he could. Not when Justin still needed him so much.

"Makes sense," Harley agreed.

Ryker finished typing. "There. Now, let's go see Adele and her shoeing. Then we should hit the road. *Oui?*"

Harley smiled and nodded. *"Oui."*

"Well, lunch first somewhere." His stomach grumbled. "Then back to Opulence."

She smiled sweetly. "I think we can make that work. David has already mentioned wanting us to stay. If you're up for that?"

"I think that's fair."

Ryker followed her out of the treatment room, disposing of his gown. There were so many things to love about this area. So many good things, yet he was so terrified of making the leap. But he wasn't as scared of taking that chance as he was when he first came here.

Maybe, just maybe, Opulence could be his and Justin's home too.

CHAPTER FOURTEEN

WHEN DAVID HAD insisted on making them lunch, Harley honestly thought that he was going to make something simple and quick. But when the grill came out and David got cooking, Ryker was completely invested in it and didn't seem to be in such a rush. Not that she could blame him.

David was an amazing cook.

They ate outside the small ranch house, overlooking the farm. David and Armand's ranch was on a hilltop, so they could see a thin blue line of Lake Huron in the distance and all the other surrounding farms. It was one of the most beautiful spots in this area, although she naturally preferred her farm.

Then again, David had over a thousand acres and she just had thirty…but dogs didn't need a thousand acres to run like horses did.

As the lunch went on Harley could see the big, dark, rolling shelf clouds coming over the western horizon and the lake. There were more warnings popping up on her phone, only now it was more serious and there was a potential threat for a tornado and localized flooding.

Ryker and she quickly packed up and said their goodbyes, but the storm rolled in quicker than Harley could drive. Not far into the journey, they were blasted with heavy, torrential downpour making visibility very difficult.

"How far does this storm spread?" Ryker asked. She could hear the concern in his voice. She knew he was thinking about Justin.

She was too.

"It's across most of northern Huron County and western Bruce County," she replied. "It's coming in from Michigan across the lake."

Ryker's phone dinged and he glanced at it. "Michel and Maureen are at your place with Justin. The go-karting got rained out. Justin is upset, but Willow is calming him. I hope you don't mind, Michel used your spare key. The tiny house is kind of cramped."

"Not at all." Harley was glad Willow was calming Justin down and most likely vice versa. Willow wasn't a big fan of thunderstorms. She could tell by the way Ryker's brow furrowed and how he kept checking his phone that he was increasingly worried about Justin.

"I shouldn't have stayed for lunch," he murmured.

"We still might've been caught in it," Harley admitted. "It came in fast."

"I was just enjoying myself. Adult conversations, good food…" He trailed off.

"You don't need to apologize."

A bolt of sheet lightning arched across the sky,

along with a crack of thunder that seemed to shake her truck.

"That was close," she murmured. There was a greenish tint to the sky, and it was darkening the closer they got to the lake. She wouldn't be surprised if waterspouts developed.

The wind picked up and had a hollow, eerie whistle to it.

Ryker's phone and hers went off at the same time. Warning alerts telling everyone in their area to seek shelter now.

The rain blasted them sideways, and it became hard to keep control of the truck. She couldn't see through the rain. They were already thirty minutes from David's and forty minutes from home.

"We need to take shelter," Ryker stated, his face hardened.

"I think you're right." As they passed a gravel side road, a bolt of lightning struck a tree, which fell down in front of them.

Harley slammed on the brakes, her truck hydro-planing before coming to a stop.

"You okay?" Ryker asked.

"Yep. My heart rate should return to normal soon," she said, nervously trying to make light of their near miss. "The road to my parents' cottage is a few minutes back the way we came. We can wait out the storm there."

"Good idea." Ryker texted Michel to tell him.

Calming her frazzled nerves, Harley turned the

truck around and made her way back a few minutes to the private road that she knew led down the hill to a cluster of cottages. Her parents' place was at the end. Navigating other fallen branches, she made it to her parents' cottage, parked her truck and dug out the spare key on her key ring. Then they made a mad dash to the front door through the pelting rain that was turning to hail.

Her fingers were cold and numb as she unlocked the door, the wind pushing them both inside. By the time they got in and shut the door against the strong wind, they were absolutely drenched.

"Let's see if we have electricity." Harley flicked on the light switch and it did nothing. "Nope."

"Well, at least we have a roof."

The wind howled and the thunder rumbled. They both stared up at the roof nervously, half expecting it to be blown off. There was a crash, and they rushed to the window to see that an old spruce had fallen down, blocking the driveway and the road, and narrowly avoiding hitting Harley's truck.

Great.

They were trapped here.

"I need to tell Justin I'm okay, but that I'll be delayed." Ryker pulled out his phone but cussed, and she saw he had no service. She pulled out her phone and saw she had no bars either.

"Try the old rotary," Harley suggested as she looked for towels and blankets in the linen closet.

"Bonne." Ryker picked up the phone, but there

was a loud crackle of static, which meant the phone line had been struck by lightning.

"Put it down!" Harley shouted, suddenly remembering you shouldn't use a landline phone during a thunderstorm. The risk was small, but if lightning struck it, he could get shocked.

"*Tabarnak*," he cursed, setting it down quickly. "I wanted to tell them I was safe and where I was."

"Michel, Maureen and Willow are with him. He'll be fine."

Ryker nodded apprehensively, but she could tell he was nervous. She handed him towels and a blanket. "*Quoi?*"

"I'm not sitting around in wet clothes. Modesty be damned," she muttered.

"Agreed. We're adults."

"Exactly. You can use the guest bedroom and I'll go into my parents'. Maybe they have some dry clothes here."

"*Merci.*"

She slipped into her parents' room and got out of her wet denim. She took it all off, because she was completely soaked through. The storm was raging and the wind was howling. She could see the small trees in the yard bent over under the unrelenting wind. It was so dark in her parents' wood-paneled homage to the eighties cottage, that she fumbled.

There were no spare clothes, so instead she wrapped herself up in a quilt and grabbed an emergency flashlight to make her way back to the living room.

Ryker was there. A towel wrapped around his waist. His broad, muscular chest was bare. Her pulse began to race and she tried not to look at him, but it was hard not to.

"Any luck?" he asked, obviously referring to clothes.

"Nope. Nothing. The one time my parents don't have anything." She shuffled toward the couch, shivering. He came and sat close to her, the two of them just sitting there and listening to the storm rage. It wasn't the only storm raging though; her own storm was raging in the very fiber of her being.

Her body was so very aware of how close he was and how alone they were.

"The OPP will come check the cottages here," she said, breaking the silence. "Once the storm is over."

"I hope service is returned soon so I can call Justin."

"I'm sure it will be," she reassured him gently.

Ryker sighed. "I would hate for this to set him back. He's made great strides here. He's more himself."

"And how about you?" she asked.

"What do you mean?"

"You're so concerned for Justin, but have *you* been able to heal, too?"

They had talked about this before, about healing. She had thought she was good, but just spending time with him, she was beginning to realize she was also on her own journey of trusting again. Only she wasn't completely there.

She was falling in love with him, of that she was certain, but she wasn't sure she could trust him not to leave her.

He sighed. "I've never really had a moment to process it all. Justin and his mental health have been my priority, but…yes. I think I have," Ryker admitted, his voice shaking. "I grieved my wife's loss, but my everything was Justin. When we first came here, I wasn't sure what I should feel. I'd just been so numb for so long. I think that being here has helped."

Harley understood that. She'd gone through the same thing with Jason when he left her standing there in her wedding dress. Hurt, crushed and humiliated. It had taken her a while to find herself, to get the strength and courage to move on and to protect her heart and set boundaries.

Boundaries that she and Ryker seemed to cross every time they were together. Her walls kept everyone out but him, it seemed. So when he said that Opulence could heal him, her heart was hopeful.

"What about you?" Ryker asked. "Has Opulence helped your heart heal?"

"I'd like to think so."

"You're not sure?"

"Are you?" she asked.

He shrugged. "You don't date?"

"No."

"Why?" Ryker asked.

"At first I told myself it was because I was too busy, but maybe that was because I was scared of being hurt again. Both were true, because the reality is my business took all my focus. There's not much downtime. But I've also learned that people never stay in Opulence. Not really. It's small, but that doesn't bother me. There's just not a lot of single men around here. I have to be careful. I'm not going to lower my standards because I'm lonely."

She was completely rambling, giving him a thousand excuses why she was alone, but in reality it was fear. Fear of having her life decided for her. Fear of being abandoned and alone. "My choice was taken from me. My ex decided to end our relationship because he changed his mind about where he wanted to live, and he assumed I wouldn't be happy with him in the city. He didn't give me a voice, so it's been better to be alone. I make my own decisions."

Except during these weeks with Ryker, she realized that wasn't true.

"Are you lonely?"

"I am," she admitted.

Ryker nodded. "I am lonely too."

"It's nice to have a friend though." Their gazes locked and her heart was racing, her body began to thrum with need as she thought about their kiss and every touch they'd shared since.

How she melted for him.

Every moment they spent together, she thought about how she wasn't alone when she was with him.

Thunder crashed again, the wind and rain lashing at the cottage, but she couldn't really hear it over her own hammering heart. She longed for him to wrap his arms around her, to hold her close.

To make her feel safe again.

Ryker reached out and brushed a damp curl of hair from her face. "It is nice to have a friend. Or maybe more than a friend…"

"Yes," she whispered.

"I would like to kiss you, Harley," Ryker said. "I know we said it was a one-time—"

"I would like that too," she interrupted him.

"You're not babbling," he whispered, leaning closer. "No longer talking a mile a minute like you usually do when you're nervous."

"I'm not nervous now." And she wasn't, because this was what she wanted. This was serious. She moved closer and reached out to touch his face, her hand trembling. He took her hand and pressed a hot, searing kiss on the pulse point of her wrist, making a zing of liquid pleasure shoot up her arm.

She wanted to resist him, but it had been so long.

She wanted to feel vulnerable with someone. To be held and have that kind of intimate connection she had denied herself in order to protect her heart.

She didn't know what was going to happen after, but it could just be about now. This moment.

Just about connection and comfort.

This was something she wanted. Something she'd been fighting since she met him. She just wanted to be carried away in his arms, in his embrace.

Sure, her heart might be broken at the end of this, but it was a risk she was willing to take to feel something again. She cupped his face, pulling him close, the blanket falling away from her shoulders to reveal her nakedness. Harley pressed her lips against his and melted into his kiss.

Sweet and honeyed.

And completely overwhelming.

It rocked her to her core and she never wanted this to end. Their kiss deepened and his hands were in her hair as he pressed her down into the couch. She was ready, and she wanted this stolen moment of passion with Ryker.

Her desire for him was fierce. It scared her all over again because she'd never felt this way for another man. Not even Jason. But she had to live in this moment. "Ryker, I want you."

"Harley, I don't think we can," he murmured. "I want to, but I don't have protection."

"I'm on the pill. It's okay." She pulled him close again and he cupped her breast. "Touch me."

Ryker moaned and captured her lips with his, sealing her fate. There was no turning back now and she didn't want to. His lips trailed over her body, leaving a trail of fire as she arched against him, not wanting the connection of heat to break.

She was glad for the storm, so that they didn't have clothes in their way. They were just skin to skin, heartbeat to heartbeat.

Touching.

Melting.

She ran her hands over him. Touching him as he stroked and kissed her, making her ache with need.

"You make me feel alive again," he murmured against her neck.

"*Oui.*" She whispered teasingly and he chuckled. His eyes twinkling in the shadows cast by the storm. Only flashes of lightning allowed her glimpses of his hard, muscular body over hers.

She was lost to him.

Harley opened her legs for him to settle between her thighs. She was wet and ready for him.

So very ready.

She wanted him to take her. She wanted to feel all of him inside her. She wanted him to heal her and to wipe away the past hurts. Arching her back, bucking her hips, she let him know how much she needed him. His hands branded her skin where he touched her, where he stroked between her legs making her thighs tremble.

"You are so wet," he murmured, touching her between her legs, making her burn with need as a coil of pleasure unfurled in her belly.

"I want you," she said again, breathlessly.

"J'ai tellement envie de toi." He blew across the skin of her neck. "I want you so much."

He covered her body with his, his hands pinning her wrists over her head as he licked her nipples. Their gazes locked as he slowly pushed into her, agonizingly slow.

She cried out, emotions of pleasure overwhelming her.

"You are so warm, wet and *tu es si tendu*," he moaned.

Harley moved her hips, urging him to take her harder and faster. To completely possess her. It scared her how much she wanted him. He let go of her wrists, bracing himself as he thrust faster. She dug her nails into his shoulders, clinging to him as he rode her urgently.

The sweet release was just at the edge, building deep inside her. She locked her legs around his waist as the climax washed over her and she succumbed to the wave of pleasure.

He moaned, and it wasn't long before he joined her in his own release.

She rolled to her side so he wouldn't fall off the edge of the couch. He touched her face, smiling at her so gently. She felt safe with him, but she couldn't tell him that. Instead, she ran her hands through his dark hair, tears stinging her eyes.

It was all so overpowering. The rush of emotions she had worked so hard to lock away for so long. It was like a dam had burst inside her.

"Are you crying, *cherie*?" Ryker asked.

"I'm fine," she said, her voice trembling. "It's just been so long since I..."

He nodded his head and kissed the tip of her nose. "*Oui*. I understand."

She brushed her tears away. "I don't regret what happened."

"Me either," he agreed, then he pulled her close, kissing her and holding her as she trembled against him.

She had sworn she wouldn't put expectations on this, that she could live in the moment. She had to protect her heart. The problem was her heart was already losing itself to a man who couldn't promise her forever. With Ryker, that moment had meant everything, and it was breaking her heart, the idea that he'd leave with Justin and the little family she'd gained would be gone.

The family she didn't know she needed, but had always wanted.

Ryker couldn't believe what had just happened. It had been so freeing that he had shared something so intimate with Harley. He'd never thought that he would ever share a moment like that again with anyone.

His whole life had been focused on taking care of Justin and easing his pain that he locked his own life away, his own feelings. He had been numb for so long. It was good to share something like that with someone like Harley, but there was a part of him that was scared too.

When she had trembled in his arms after it was over and he held her, he started feeling that trepidation of what would happen next. Neither of them had promised each other anything, and he wasn't sure what he could give her, because he still wasn't sure what was going to happen at the end of the summer.

He wasn't sure that he could make his and Justin's life work here, but he wanted it to.

He loved his friendship with Harley, he loved working with her and spending time with her. He'd already suspected he was falling in love with her, but now he knew that he couldn't stop it.

"So what do we do?" she asked.

"We wait." He wasn't sure if that's what she wanted to hear, but he didn't know what to say. He was healing, but was he ready to take a chance on a big move? One that would affect his son? He wasn't sure.

"Do you really need to leave Opulence?" she asked.

It caught him off guard.

"Montreal is home," he admitted. "It would be hard to leave there. You could visit in Montreal."

"I could, though my farm takes time and it's hard to leave for long."

"True. I have thought about moving here, more than once, but it's such a big decision."

"Understandable. It's hard to make a change."

"*Oui*," he replied tightly.

There was a buzz and then the lights turned on.

"We have power!" Harley exclaimed, jumping up. "I'm throwing our clothes in the dryer."

"That's a good idea." Ryker pulled out his phone, but there was still no service.

Tabarnak.

He was concerned that Justin would be having anxiety about being separated during a violent storm, and he had a bit of guilt for getting lost in the moment with Harley.

He wandered over to the window and stared outside. He could see everything clearly now. There were branches and trees all over the road, but Harley's truck still looked intact. Hopefully the storm wasn't building to a tornado. Or if it was, it didn't hit the farm.

"There, in about twenty minutes our clothes will be dry," Harley remarked, covering herself with a blanket again. "Do you have cell service yet?"

"No." He frowned. "I'm sure he's okay."

"I'm sure he is too. Try not to worry." She glanced

at her phone. "Hey, I have service. Want to call Michel with my phone and check on the farm?"

"Oui!" He took Harley's phone and called Michel.

"Harley!" Michel answered, a frantic edge to his voice.

"No. It's me, Ryker," Ryker responded. "My phone still doesn't have service. Is everything okay?"

"No," Michel said. He sounded like he was fighting back tears. "Where are you?"

"We're at Harley's parents' cottage. Outside Inverhuron. What's wrong?" Ryker was bracing himself to hear that there'd been damage to the farm or someone was injured. His mind was running amok, and he felt the same way that he had years ago when he found Daphne unconscious on the kitchen floor.

Powerless.

Helpless.

"When we couldn't get ahold of you, Justin slipped out of the house. Willow followed him, but they're missing." Ryker's stomach dropped to the soles of his feet, and he was having a hard time processing what Michel was telling him. "We went out in the storm, but I don't know where they've gone. The OPP are here, and emergency crews. We need you here, Ryker."

"I'm coming," he said without a second thought. But he swore when he remembered. "The road here is blocked."

"I'll tell the officer where you are and they'll come for you both. I'm sorry, Ryker," Michel sobbed. "I shouldn't have let him out of my sight. I can't lose him…not like I lost Daphne."

Ryker's chest constricted. He was so worried Michel would have another heart attack like he did when his daughter died. "It's not your fault. I will be there as soon as I can. We'll be waiting for the OPP."

He hung up the phone, handed it back to Harley and ran his fingers through his hair, not sure of what to do. It felt like his knees were giving out.

He couldn't lose Justin.

Maybe this change for the summer was a mistake. Maybe it had been too much. He shouldn't have pushed for Justin to be independent of him. He should've gone go-karting with his son.

"What's wrong?" Harley asked.

"Justin panicked and ran away…with Willow. They can't find them. They were lost in the storm."

Harley gasped. "Oh my God."

"The OPP are coming to get us." Ryker swallowed the hard lump in his throat as all this anger just bubbled up inside him. "I should've never come here. I should've never taken him from Montreal. This was all a mistake. I can't stay here."

He saw the look of hurt in Harley's eyes. He didn't mean that she was a mistake, but he couldn't tell her that, because all he could think about was getting to his son, whom he shouldn't have left.

He moved past her to stand in front of the dryer, where he panicked in silence and watched the load spin until it dinged and he could get his clothes.

The moment they found Justin, he was heading back to Montreal and the safety of their small home. He would make sure that Justin would always feel safe. He should've gone go-karting with his son today, or he at least should've stayed at the tiny home.

Hell, he should've stayed in Montreal. Where it was just the two of them. A place where he could keep an eye on Justin. Montreal was their home, and it helped him in this frantic moment to visualize bringing his son back there safely, but somewhere behind the panic in his mind, for the first time, it didn't feel so much like home when he thought about it. Knowing it would be just him and Justin alone.

CHAPTER FIFTEEN

THE RIDE BACK to her farm in the OPP cruiser was silent. Ryker was understandably stressed, as was she. She'd known it was likely that he wouldn't stay, and this incident would definitely drive him away. She couldn't blame him. It hurt so much because despite her best efforts to keep Ryker at arm's length, she had fallen in love with him.

With both him and his son.

Right now, she was having a hard time trying to keep it all together, because she was hurt, but scared and angry too. Angry that they weren't there for Justin and that he was so afraid he ran away. Like his dad, Justin had sort of worked his way under her skin and into her heart. She worried about Justin and Willow. Maybe it was foolish, but her little dog had been her whole world for so long.

As they drove back to her farm, she could see the downed hydro lines and there was a small path in a field of destruction where something had touched down, but none of that would be confirmed until later.

She just hoped that they could find Justin and Willow. That the two of them hadn't wandered far. It was still raining pretty heavily, and the temperature had dropped by the time they pulled onto her property.

Kaitlyn was there, with a few of their clients and some other volunteers from town.

Michel was standing in the rain as the cruiser pulled up. His face was drawn and haggard. As the OPP officer parked, Ryker got out of the back without saying a word to her and went straight to Michel and Maureen. She followed him and noticed Maureen was openly sobbing. Her arm was bandaged in a sling and there were paramedics on the scene.

"It's my fault," Maureen said, weeping.

"How?" Ryker asked, gently touching her shoulder.

"He saw me get hurt. I slipped and came down hard on my arm. Then he cried out for Willow to come back and…he took off. I tried to chase him, but the wind was so strong," Maureen whimpered.

"We've searched all the buildings, no sign of him," an officer said.

"How about the forest?" Harley suggested. "There's seventeen acres and he's always been fascinated by it. He told me about how he'd like to visit it."

The officer nodded. "We're going to start there, but…"

"What?" Ryker asked, an edge to his voice.

"The creek is overflowing and the footbridge over the creek to the forest is moving fast. We can't get over the footbridge. There's water with a strong current running over the top."

Maureen cried out and Michel pulled her close. Harley's heart sank.

Ryker's eyes were wild and he began to cuss as Harley paced around the yard in the rain. She knew exactly what the OPP officer was suggesting, that Justin and Willow were both swept away. She swallowed a lump in her throat. She didn't want to think about it.

"There's a higher water crossing, farther down about seven kilometers at the side road," Harley suggested. "It's a direct line into my forest, and the water wouldn't be going over that bridge."

"We should go," Ryker suggested.

The officer nodded. "Let's go. He'll be wet and the temperatures are dropping fast. We don't want hypothermia to set in."

They formed a search party.

Michel and Maureen stayed behind, with Kaitlyn and Sarah looking after them. Harley changed into her rubber boots and threw a raincoat on, giving Ryker boots and a raincoat too. They didn't say anything; there was nothing to say in this moment. She knew he wasn't staying. Nothing would change that now.

She saw this coming. It just sucked that she was right all along and ignored her instincts anyways.

Right now though, all that mattered was finding Justin.

The emergency crews gave them reflective gear and flashlights, and they all drove over to the side road, seven kilometers away, while other rescue crews searched the creek flats.

She didn't want to consider the possibility that something worse had happened, because she didn't believe it for one moment. Justin and Willow were fine. They would be okay.

Once they got to the high water crossing, they made their way through the fields and then they split up. Everyone was calling Justin's name.

"As soon as I find him, we're heading home," Ryker groused.

"He'll be fine," Harley reassured him. "Then maybe if you give it a couple of days—"

"I'm in no mood, Harley," Ryker snapped, cutting her off. "This trip was a bad idea. I let my guard down because Justin seemed happy."

"He *is* happy here," Harley countered.

"And what would you know? You're not a parent. Opulence isn't safe for a child, but you don't believe that because you only see the perfection of Opulence. You're just too afraid to leave."

She knew Ryker was just afraid for his son, and lashing out, but it hurt, because it was true. She wasn't a parent. But she wasn't scared of leaving Opulence.

Aren't you?

She couldn't leave. Her business was here. She was so connected to this place because yes, maybe Opulence had always been her safety net, but it was good to her too. Her life was here, and she wasn't looking to change anything.

"And Montreal is so perfect?" she asked. "I think you use Justin as an excuse not to take a chance on something. I'm not the only one afraid."

Ryker didn't say anything to her, but he started down one forest path and she headed in a different direction, straight into the middle of her forest, fuming and upset.

The bush lot was owned by several land owners in the area, and she knew exactly where the boundaries of her forest lay. She knew that if he went too far in one direction, there was a steep drop-off, back into the creek flats that wound their way through several properties before joining the main river that flowed toward Lake Huron.

She hoped that Justin wasn't too scared to come when his name was being called by a stranger. She could hear the distant pleadings, calls for Justin, calls for Willow echoing through the forest.

When Justin had stayed over at her house, she had told him in the center of her forest was an old truck and a tree house. He had been fascinated by that. She only hoped that he'd headed there, because that's where she was leading them.

"Justin!" she cried out. "Willow?" She whistled, hoping her little dog would let her know they were nearby. She climbed over branches and fallen trees. It was still raining, and thick droplets from the canopy of trees were sliding down the back of her neck, but she didn't care.

It seemed like the slowest walk ever when she finally caught sight of the truck and the tree house. She shined her flashlight onto the muddy forest floor and saw where small shoes had imprinted the ground, followed by paw prints. They'd almost been washed away by the rain, but they were still faintly visible.

Her heart skipped a beat as she found shoes, stuck in the mud, and socks that were soaked. The footsteps still made their way toward the drop-off, so she quickened her pace. Calling for them.

"Justin! Willow!"

Then she heard it.

A weak bark.

Faint.

She ran, branches scratching her face as she headed to the drop-off. It was getting darker, and another storm would soon start rolling through.

"Willow!" She paused at the edge and heard the barking again, looking down she saw Willow there, sitting on top of an unconscious Justin, who was caught up on branches. His coat snagged and his head was next to a rock. She could see he was injured, but the rock and branch had stopped him from sliding into the rushing water below.

"Oh, God," she gasped.

Willow couldn't climb the steep hill and she was whining something fierce. Muddied and shivering.

"Stay there, girl. Keep him safe. Help is coming." She pulled out the flare gun an OPP officer had given her earlier, found a clearing and fired a flare into the sky to let the rescue crew know where she was.

Ryker was panicking inside. His voice was hoarse from calling Justin's name, and all he could do was beat himself up for bringing him here.

Why did he bring him here?

That's what he was asking himself over and over again. Then he thought of Harley and all the mean things he'd said when he was scared and afraid. He regretted it because he was falling for her. Was he willing to admit that now? He still felt hesitant about his feelings. If only she'd consider leaving Opulence, maybe they could work something out. Was that true? Or would he still need time to figure out his feelings? The thing was, she wouldn't be happy in the city.

He knew that.

He saw the flare and heard the pop. His heart rose into his throat, and he started to make his way over to the source. He wasn't far.

Please let him be alive. Please.

He broke through the brush and saw Harley there, standing over the edge of a drop-off.

God. No.

"Harley?" he asked frantically.

"I found him. They're stuck," she explained.

Ryker ran to the edge and saw his son, bleeding but safe from the rushing water below. Willow was muddied and sitting on him, protecting him the best she could. He frantically looked around, trying to find some way that he could get down there and retrieve them, but it was so steep and muddy. He didn't want to knock Justin loose and have him and Willow be swept away in the creek below.

That feeling of powerlessness became all too apparent again.

All he could do was wait, and it was agonizing.

Why had he left him alone today?

"Over here!" someone shouted in the distance.

Harley turned around, waving. "We're here. We found them!"

Rescue crews and officers came through the brush. Ryker stood back as Harley explained to them that Justin was hanging precariously at the bottom of a steep embankment. They had the gear to traverse the cliff.

A stretcher was brought out and the EMS crew went to work to rig up their rappelling gear to retrieve Justin and Willow.

Ryker stood next to Harley. Without thinking, he reached down and took her hand for comfort, and she squeezed it in response.

"I'm sorry for what I said earlier. I was unnecessarily harsh. But I can't stay here," he said. "We're going to go home. I know I have my own stuff to deal with, but I can't ask you to move for me while

I'm still processing everything. You wouldn't be happy in the city. I know that. So you need to stay."

She frowned, her lip trembling. "You're not giving me a choice either way."

"It's for the best," he stated firmly.

He was hurting her, but it was to protect her in the long run.

She pulled her hand away as Justin was lifted to safety and put on the stretcher. Ryker was by the paramedics' side as they lifted the stretcher up and carried it through the brush to a clearing.

Justin was alive.

Injured, but alive.

Harley made her way to the edge as a member of the rescue crew went down and brought back up a very muddy and upset cockapoo.

Tears streamed down Harley's face as she took her sweet little lamb of a dog in her arms. "Good girl."

Willow was trembling, but licking her face.

A paramedic handed her a blanket. "She did good."

Harley nodded and wrapped her dog up, holding her close while they worked to stabilize Justin. He was still unconscious, hypothermic and probably had a concussion. They lifted the stretcher out and took him to the edge of the forest, where the ambulance was waiting, thanks to her neighbor, a farmer, who led them down the lane that he had made for retrieving wood. They got Justin into the back of the ambulance and Ryker followed. He glanced back at Harley, standing there with Willow.

The dog howled mournfully and Harley just kissed her muddy little head. She was shivering now too, and he wanted her to come with him. She could come to Montreal too, but what could he give her there? He made the choice for her, so she wouldn't resent him in the end.

She had a business here. Her family. Her farm. Her animals.

There was nothing he could offer her.

Your heart?

Only he wasn't sure that was enough. It was better to end it before it began and not give her a real choice.

It has begun already. You're a fool. He shook that thought away.

The paramedics closed the doors between them. The lights and siren went on, and he just sat in the back as the paramedics worked on Justin. They were going to the children's hospital in London.

All that mattered right now was his son. Not his heart. Just the safety and security of Justin. He'd been foolish to think that a summer here would help them heal. Justin still needed him, and he was done trying to push Justin out his comfort zone.

He had what he needed.

He had had love before and he was greedy to think that he could have a second shot at it. He just hoped that when all was said and done, when the dust settled, Harley would forgive him. As much as he had fallen in love with her, and he had, he hoped that she would still want to be his friend, even if he couldn't properly give her his heart like he wanted to.

Even though he'd hurt her.

Harley held Willow tight on the ride back to the farm. The OPP officer helped her out, and it felt like her legs were going to collapse under her. When she got there, Michel was waiting. Her phone rang and she saw it was her brother calling.

Harley choked back a sob. "Hey."

"It'll be okay," David replied. Michel came up behind her and put his arms around her shoulders.

"How did you know to call?" she asked.

"The storm. I was worried. I called the house and Michel answered and told me what happened. He said you found them."

"Yes. I'm glad you called," Harley sobbed. "I've got to go. Call me back in a bit."

"I love you, Nerd," David said gently.

"Ditto." She ended the call and saw Christine coming her way with a blanket. She was grateful for her friends.

"They told us you found Justin, a few minutes before you got back," Michel said weakly.

Harley nodded. "They're taking him to the Children's Hospital of Western Ontario in London."

Michel nodded. "Thank God you found him and that Willow was with him. What a good girl."

Willow was still trembling.

"Let me take her. I can take a look at our little hero," Michel insisted.

"I'll help," Kaitlyn offered.

Harley nodded as Michel took Willow from her arms, which were frozen and numb. She looked at Christine, shaking still.

"You're cold and wet. We need to get you warm too," Christine said. "Maureen is resting inside and Michel has Willow. Let me take care of you, like you take care of our pets."

Harley broke down sobbing. She couldn't hold back the rush of emotions anymore. She had cried in private when Jason had left her, but then she stopped crying and continued to make a life for herself, determined to prove to everyone that she was okay. And she was eventually, but right now her heart was breaking all over again, and she couldn't hide that.

She loved Ryker and she had loved Justin, but she'd been having a hard time seeing how it could all work out, even if Ryker hadn't bailed. Maybe it was a good thing Ryker didn't give her a choice either, so she wouldn't be so brokenhearted if it ended when they were in even deeper.

It still hurt though.

It still broke her heart. It angered her to not have that choice. Again.

Christine led her into the house and took her straight upstairs, into her bathroom. Even though Harley was a grown woman, Christine drew her a bath and then helped her out of her wet clothes. It had been so long since she had let someone take care of her.

Harley settled into the bath, but was still shaking. "Christine, can I have my phone? It's in my jacket."

"Sure." Christine left and brought her the phone and shut the bathroom door. She called her brother back, her hand trembling.

"Nerd?" David asked softly.

"I did it again."

"What?" David asked.

"I've fallen in love with the wrong man." She sobbed. "I've fallen in love with his son and—"

"He's not the wrong man, Harley. Jason was. You didn't cry this much when Jason left you. Don't let Ryker go. You need those two as much as they need you."

"But he's leaving…"

"Not everything has to be decided today."

"Okay," she whispered.

"You're okay. As soon as the road opens, I'll be there."

"Thanks."

"Rest, and call again if you need me, sis."

"Will do." Harley ended the call and set her phone down on the vanity.

She sat in the hot bath for a while, until she

stopped shaking. She got up and dried herself off. She put on warm clothes from the dryer and made her way into the kitchen. Maureen was sitting at the table, and Harley went over to her and kissed her cheek.

"You saved them," Maureen said.

"Hardly, I just found them."

Maureen looked at her seriously. "Trust me when I say you saved them."

Harley's throat constricted. "Ryker said he's going back to Montreal."

"Because he's mad at himself," Michel said, coming back into the house with Willow, who had been freshly cleaned and dried by Kaitlyn. Willow limped over to her, whining. Harley scooped up her little dog.

"Is she okay?" Harley asked.

"She's sprained a tendon. I gave her some painkillers. She'll be fine. She's a hero," Michel proclaimed.

Harley buried her face in Willow's fur.

No one said anything. Christine placed a cup of tea in front of her, while Willow curled up on her lap. Michel took a seat and sighed.

"It felt like we'd lost Daphne all over again," he said, his voice breaking. "Daphne would be so grateful to you, for finding Justin. We all are. And I think Daphne would want you to keep taking care of Justin. We all love you and Justin adores you. He's told us. You're exactly what Ryker and Justin need. Ryker is angry and scared, and I can't blame him for that, but the worst thing for them would be to go back to Montreal. He doesn't have family there, and Justin loves it here. Both of Ryker's parents are gone. You can be his family, Harley."

Maureen reached out. "Be a part of our family."

"I'm not sure if I'm brave enough for that," she said, her voice trembling. "Or that my life here is what Ryker wants."

"It is," Maureen said. "Don't let my stubborn son-in-law go. Justin and he need you, and Daphne would want it that way."

"You've felt so alone since Jason left you, and he wasn't right for you," Christine said. "You aren't alone, Harley, and you don't have to do this life alone. Love means hurt sometimes, but it's also joy and happiness. When you're ready, go, get your family."

Harley nodded.

She was scared to take a chance on going to London and telling Ryker how she felt about him and Justin, but if she didn't take the chance, she would regret it for the rest of her life. Ryker and Justin belonged here, but most important, she belonged with them.

Her little family.

Even if it meant she had to go to Montreal and prove it.

She was tired of being alone because she was too afraid to reach out and take a chance. She'd been brave about a lot of things in her life, but love was something she was always scared of. Even now, looking back, she had been scared about the unknowns with Jason, and when he left her at the altar it just confirmed all her worst fears.

It was enough of an impetus to say that she was never going to fall in love again. It was enough of an excuse to close herself off from others, from love. She thought she had protected her heart well, but she was wrong.

It wasn't protection.

It was loneliness. It was giving up on dreams.

It was hurt.

She'd taken a chance to make the rest of her dreams come true. She couldn't back away from this dream, her long secret dream of a family.

Of happiness.

Of love.

This was her second chance, and she wasn't going to let it pass her by, because if she did she would regret it for the rest of her life.

He may have thought he took away her choice, but he didn't.

She was going to fight to take back the decision he made for her, because losing the both of them wasn't in her best interest.

Ryker had spent the night in an uncomfortable hospital chair in Justin's room. Actually, it was a leather reclining chair. It wasn't horrible as far as hospital rooms went. Justin had roused, but he was still suffering from the effects of hypothermia, and he had a concussion.

The pediatric doctors planned to keep Justin in the hospital for a few days. Ryker had texted Michel to give him an update and asked if he could bring down a change of clothes and Justin's blanket that Harley had made.

His heart sank as he thought about Harley.

He was in love with her, and he'd hurt her by pushing her away because he was scared.

When that ambulance pulled away and his last view of her was her standing there holding Willow, he could see her heart was breaking, just as much as his.

Ryker never thought that he would ever find love again, but he had.

It was tearing him up knowing that he would have to leave her, because he couldn't ask her to leave Opulence. He'd pushed her to the side and took away her choice, her voice, like a fool. *Just like her ex.*

When he had heard what happened to her with her ex, he couldn't even fathom someone doing that to someone they professed to love. It wasn't right, and he swore that he wouldn't ever be like that, but here he was.

Ending it before it really even began.

And it was just an excuse. He was using Harley's love of Opulence as an excuse to end things, but really it was his own fear. Fear of losing someone special again… But he'd already lost her by pushing her away. *Tabarnak!* He'd really messed up.

"Pappa?" Justin moaned.

Ryker sat up and went to his son's bedside. He took his little hand in his. "I'm here."

Justin opened his eyes. "My head hurts."

"You had a fall. Remember?"

Justin blinked. "Willow?"

"She's okay."

"She fell down that embankment. I was just trying to get back home," Justin whispered, tears running slowly down his cheeks.

"To Montreal?"

Justin frowned. "No, to the farm. Home. We both were."

"That's not our home though," Ryker said softly. "We're going to go home to Montreal."

"I don't want to go back there," Justin cried.

"Justin, you ran away when I wasn't there."

"No! I saw Nanna get hurt and then Willow got out and she bolted so fast, but then I caught up to her and the storm was too bad. I was scared, but Harley told me there was a tree house. I couldn't see how to get back to the farm, so I took Willow to find the tree house."

"You weren't running because I was away?" Ryker asked.

Justin looked sheepish. "At first, but like I said…

thunder and lightning and I guess both Willow and I got scared."

"It's okay." Ryker stroked his face. "All that matters is you're okay. I shouldn't have been apart from you."

"Pappa, I'm okay here," Justin said vehemently. "I want to stay in Opulence. Mom is here."

"Justin," Ryker said quietly.

"I know Mom is gone, but I feel her here. Gramps and Nanna love Harley and so do I. I want a family again, Pappa, and I want you back…the way you were. The way we used to be." Tears were rolling down Justin's face. "I want to be near Gramps and Nanna. I'm happy here. Can we stay? You can take over Gramps's practice and I can go to school in Londesborough. Gramps showed me the school. It looks so nice."

Ryker began to cry. Wiping his tears away, he asked, "You're sure this is what you want?"

"I don't want to forget Mom and here I won't. Please can we stay? Maybe Harley will let us stay in her tiny home."

"Hi," a small voice said from the open door. Ryker spun around to see Harley standing there, holding a small duffel bag and a very worn blanket in her hands. His heart swelled and he had to fight back tears again, just seeing her there. Safe and sound.

She had come all this way for them. Maybe he hadn't ruined it all when he pushed her away.

"Harley!" Justin exclaimed.

Harley held up his blanket. "I thought you might need this."

"My blanket!" Justin began to cry. "Harley, I'm sorry."

"No need to apologize." She tousled his hair gently. "I'm glad you're okay."

"And Willow?" he asked.

"She was muddy, but your Gramps took care of her. You saved her and she saved you. You're best friends forever. I'm sure of it."

Justin smiled and snuggled his face into his blanket. "I'm really tired."

"Rest then, buddy," Ryker said gently. He touched his face. "I'll just be outside the door."

Ryker motioned for Harley to follow. She followed, with one last look at Justin. When they were in the hall he closed the door, just slightly.

"You brought him his blanket," he said quietly.

"He needs it. Besides, it's the best blanket ever." She smiled. "I was worried. I care about him. A lot."

"I know."

Her eyes were filling with tears. "Look, Ryker. I know you said you have to go back to Montreal but…don't. Not because I'm afraid to leave, but because you both belong here. And you know what, if you can't stay… I don't know how things will work, but we'll figure something out, because I can't lose either one of you. I love you. I love Justin."

Ryker brushed away her tears with his thumb. "I love you too and Justin loves you."

She nodded. "If I have to invest in Michel's clinic to keep you here or… I don't know…move to Montreal…"

He shook his head. "That won't be necessary. What I said to you, I was scared. Montreal is all I've ever known. Sure, I have a job and we have friends, but here we have a family. I was so scared about leaving my own safety net, a place where I could control and keep Justin and I both safe, but what we really need is family. It's been so long since I've had more than just Justin in my life. I took away your choice and I hope you forgive me, because I would like to date you."

"So you're staying?" she asked cautiously.

"We're going to stay, and I'll open the practice full-time, make it my own, finally."

"You mean that?" she asked.

He nodded. "*Oui.* I love you, Harley. I never thought that I would find love again, but I have. You've healed us."

"You've both healed me too. I can't picture my life without either of you," she responded. "So much so I would've gone to Montreal with you both. I would've hated it, but to be with you and Justin, it would've been worth it. You're right, Opulence isn't perfect."

"No. I was wrong. It's perfect because you're there, because it's home."

He brushed his knuckles across her cheek and then bent down to kiss her softly, pulling her into his arms. When the kiss was over, she wrapped her arms around him and rested her head on his shoulder, melting into his embrace.

"I do have a problem though," he said.

"What? Closing up everything in Montreal? That won't be a problem. I'll come help."

"No, not that. I'll need to extend my lease until I find a place."

She chuckled. "I can do that, but no rush. This is your home now."

"No. You're my home." And he kissed her again. He'd never thought he could fall in love again, but he realized now that he wasn't replacing Daphne, he was opening his heart, expanding it to include Harley.

"I have some more good news," Harley said.

Ryker was curious. *"Quoi?"*

"Sharpe Line Farms shut down. Criminal charges were laid, and their puppies and breeding dogs are now with appropriate rescues. Christine stayed with me last night and got a text about it. I was thinking, we need one of those doggos. Maybe not a puppy, but definitely a mama dog. And I might've adopted a cat."

Ryker chuckled. "Nia?"

She nodded. "Yep. You can call that adoption emotionally driven."

"Justin will be thrilled. About both the new dog and the cat."

"Well, that's the beauty of country life."

"I wouldn't have it any other way," he said.

"Pappa?" Justin called out.

"Shall we go tell him?" Harley asked.

"Yes. We'll probably have to tell it to him again later, because his head is still fuzzy from the concussion, but he'll be thrilled."

Harley nodded. "We're a family."

"*Oui.* Family. Forever."

EPILOGUE

One year later

"You need to go deal with Cluck Norris Jr.," Kaitlyn insisted as Harley finished sweeping the grooming room. Kaitlyn had her hands on her hips and was very insistent about the whole thing.

"What?" Harley asked, removing her noise canceling headphones.

Willow and her rescue mama dog, Birch, looked up from where they were snoozing on the big dog bed together. They weren't completely interested in what Kaitlyn was saying.

"Cluck Norris Jr. is out, and he's running amok across the yard!"

"What!" Harley set down her broom and headed outside.

Stupid rooster.

Justin had insisted upon handling the chickens. She just hoped she could wrangle Cluck Norris back to the pen before he became splattered across the road. She headed outside and froze in her driveway.

A bunch of people were there, and a weird archway had been erected with lights. Justin was standing in front of her in a suit.

Harley chuckled nervously. "Why are you wearing a suit and tie?"

Justin held out his hand. "It's a surprise. Everyone is in on it."

Harley glanced around the yard, and she could see her parents, Michel, Maureen, Sarah, Armand and David. Harley gasped, her heart hammering, and she spun around to see Kaitlyn standing in the doorway with Willow and Birch. There were little fancy bows on Willow's and Birch's heads.

Nia scooted by, followed by a couple of the barn cats Harley had also adopted.

Justin took her hand and led her through the yard.

Everyone was dressed up but her, and she really didn't know what was happening. She wasn't a huge fan of surprises. Ryker should know that, considering that when he snuck up on her a year ago, she'd tossed him into alpaca poo.

She glanced over at the alpaca pen, and the three alpacas were sticking their heads over the fence. Vince had a bow tie and Gozer and Zuul had bows as well.

"What's going on?" Harley asked again, her voice trembling.

"Surprise!" Justin exclaimed.

Ryker melted out of the crowd, also wearing a suit, and her heart skipped a beat as he reached out and took her hands. Behind him was Cluck Norris Jr. and the rest of the chickens. Somehow Cluck Norris Jr., Wyatt Chirp and Count Cluckula had little tuxedo vests on. That must have taken serious dedication and courage.

"I don't like surprises," she teased nervously.

"Just enjoy it, Nerd!" her brother called out.

She shot him a glare over his shoulder. Behind him was a horse-drawn carriage and Adele, the little foal from last year with the broken coffin bone was standing next to her mother who was harnessed up to it. She swallowed the lump in her throat and looked back at Ryker.

"Harley, marry me." He got down on one knee and pulled out a ring.

"All this for a proposal?" she asked, stunned.

"Well, not just a proposal. A wedding," Ryker admitted.

Harley was confused and she looked around and then down at her scrubs. "What? That is…"

"My idea," Justin said confidently. "Marry Pappa, Harley. We love you."

Tears streamed down her face. "Yes. I'll marry you."

"Bonne." Ryker cupped her face and kissed her to cheers. Justin threw his arms around them both.

"But it's not fair you're all dressed up and I'm in scrubs," she said nervously.

"Your mother has a dress," Ryker said. "Go get changed. The officiant will be here soon."

"And if I said no?" she teased.

"I bet him twenty bucks you wouldn't," Justin said. "And I was right!"

Harley laughed and pulled Justin into an embrace, kissing his head. "So you were."

Harley was whisked away by her mom, who quickly got her dressed in a simple white lace dress and did her hair. Her mom pinned a pink peony in her hair, which was her favorite flower.

Ryker and Justin had moved into the big farm house a few months after they officially started dating.

It had been the happiest year of her life.

Ryker was waiting for her under an archway that was lit up with lights. The sun was setting behind the spruce trees. Her father led her down the short little aisle to where Ryker and Justin were waiting.

Her boys.

Her family.

He wasn't leaving her. The last year had proven that. Justin was thriving at his new school. He had made so many new friends and was loving his life here.

Ryker had revitalized Michel's clinic, allowing Michel to finally fully retire, and Harley's business was booming too.

Ryker took her hands and smiled down at her. "I love you, Harley."

"I love you too."

Justin stood between them as the officiant performed a quick wedding. He handed his dad the ring, and Ryker slipped it on her finger.

"Now you can kiss her, Pappa!" Justin said, interrupting the officiant.

Ryker winked at his son and kissed her, making her melt all over again. She was finally healed, she had her family. Her dreams had all come true and they were all finally whole again, with a whole future stretched out in front of them.

For the first time, since Ryker and Justin walked into her life, she was excited about what was around the corner.

She was excited for the future with her husband, son and a farmyard full of animals at her side.

* * * * *

*If you enjoyed this story, check out
these other great reads from Amy Ruttan*

Reunited with Her Off-Limits Surgeon
Nurse's Pregnancy Surprise
Winning the Neonatal Doc's Heart
Paramedic's One-Night Baby Bombshell

All available now!